"You're the efficiency expert?"

"Yes," Emmy said.

"Are you sure?" Nick asked. No self-respecting efficiency expert would go around looking so adorable. Efficiency experts carried clipboards and stopwatches and dressed in neat suits, not skirts and sweaters. They were supposed to be all about work, not drive every thought of it from a man's mind.

Nick looked into Emmy Jones's sparkling eyes and forgot all about his plans and objections and the weight of his father's legacy. When he looked at Emmy Jones his mind went on vacation and the rest of him was left to run the show. Not good. He'd come here to get rid of the efficiency expert; kissing her wouldn't exactly accomplish that goal. And he wanted, badly, to kiss her. At least for starters…

D0778070

Dear Reader,

It's said that opposites attract, right? Well, no two people could be more opposite than Emmy Jones and Nick Porter.

Emmy loves lists, schedules, organization and planning. Sure, it's a knee-jerk reaction to having grown up in foster homes and never feeling safe and settled, but when her fiancé dumps her a month before their wedding she figures she's had a narrow escape. And she decides it's best she doesn't get married. Ever.

Nick Porter is a take-life-as-it-comes kind of guy, and what comes over him when he sees Emmy is instant attraction. He hired her to help him get his company back to profitability, but it's not long before he objects to the way she's going about it. He really doesn't like it that she refuses to admit she's just as attracted to him as he is to her. So he's going to help her get over her sad childhood by bringing some of her foster family members back to show her they weren't all bad.

It's not the best idea he's ever had, especially when the people from Emmy's past turn out to be toxic. And when Emmy's ex-fiancé returns, determined to win her back, it seems as if all the cards are stacked against Nick.

Of course, Nick and Emmy had some fun along the way, and I hope you have a great time reading their story.

Penny McCusker

Emmy and the Boss
PENNY McCUSKER

Special
Treat!

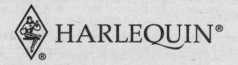

HARLEQUIN®

TORONTO • NEW YORK • LONDON
AMSTERDAM • PARIS • SYDNEY • HAMBURG
STOCKHOLM • ATHENS • TOKYO • MILAN • MADRID
PRAGUE • WARSAW • BUDAPEST • AUCKLAND

ISBN-13: 978-0-373-75200-3
ISBN-10:   0-373-75200-8

EMMY AND THE BOSS

This edition published by arrangement with Harlequin Books S.A.

® and TM are trademarks of the publisher. Trademarks indicated with
® are registered in the United States Patent and Trademark Office, the
Canadian Trade Marks Office and in other countries.

www.eHarlequin.com

Printed in U.S.A.

ABOUT THE AUTHOR

Penny McCusker is a multipublished author who lives in southeastern Michigan with her husband, three teenage kids and two dogs whose life of leisure she envies but would never be able to pull off. She's always hard at work on her next book, but she loves to hear from readers. You can contact her at pennymccusker.com.

Books by Penny McCusker

HARLEQUIN AMERICAN ROMANCE
1063—MAD ABOUT MAX
1082—NOAH AND THE STORK
1106—CRAZY FOR ELLIE

Don't miss any of our special offers. Write to us at the following address for information on our newest releases.

Harlequin Reader Service
U.S.: 3010 Walden Ave., P.O. Box 1325, Buffalo, NY 14269
Canadian: P.O. Box 609, Fort Erie, Ont. L2A 5X3

To my husband, Michael, my kids, Mike, Erin and Ian, and my large extended family. Thanks for all the love and support.

Chapter One

Emmy Jones loved lists. You could, in fact, say that lists were her life. In her estimation nothing was quite as satisfying as knowing exactly what needed to be done and checking the tasks off one by one until the list was complete, then filing it away in the neat folder in the drawer where she kept her completed lists.

Organization was big with Emmy, too.

Lists and a good filing system couldn't fix her wild blond hair—a tub of gel and a professional to apply it couldn't get her curls to lie flat and sleek—or tone down her freckles or shrink her to a more moderate height than her lanky five-foot-nine. But lists could keep her life in order, and order was something that had been in short supply in Emmy's formative years.

She believed in lists.

Lists had never failed her, and she'd never failed them. Until today.

Today, her fiancé had dumped her, making it practically impossible for her to finish her wedding list, which ended, obviously, with the actual wedding. The easiest way to solve the problem would have been to get Roger back, but she refused to do that. There were some things more important than lists—not caving in to a man who called her names, for instance. That was more important.

Rigid, he'd called her. *Inflexible.* She'd refrained from pointing out that those two words meant the same thing and the least he could do if he was dumping her was not waste her time by repeating himself. But then, it didn't take long to fling out a couple of accusations and walk out the door. Or much courage.

"I'm better off without him," she said to her best friend in the whole world, Melinda Masterson, who'd dropped whatever legal-eagle busy work she was doing to hurry into downtown Boston and keep Emmy from drinking herself into a stupor—which would have taken exactly two drinks. "He's a boring, insensitive, egotistical, boring—"

"You said boring twice."

"He's twice as boring as most people."

"I thought that was what you liked about him."

"I liked that he was dependable."

"Well, he was so dependable you could count on him to carry every conversation. Talking about himself."

"Don't remind me."

"Personally, I'm looking forward to forgetting him." Lindy took a healthy swig of her martini to kick off the process, at least in the short run. "You should be, too, Emmy. You didn't really love him."

"I kept the ring." Emmy turned the white gold engagement band with its single conservative diamond around and around on her finger, feeling her first sense of loss at the idea of taking it off. Maybe she hadn't loved Roger, but she'd liked him. He was a nice, steady, unassuming man who never demanded more of her than she was willing to give. Until this morning. Suddenly he'd wanted to know why they never held hands or spent Sunday afternoon cuddled together on the sofa. He'd wanted longing looks and secret smiles. He'd wanted sex to last more than ten minutes. She wasn't exactly the one ringing the bell on that particular alarm clock, and he thought she could do something to keep him on the job longer? Well, maybe he was right.

"He met someone else," she concluded wondering why she hadn't seen it right off the bat. He'd found a woman who'd made him realize he wanted more than the pleasant, comfortable rut they'd dug together.

"I could sue him for breach of contract. I *am* your lawyer."

"It's not worth the aggravation."

"And you don't really have any damages to claim, because if you ask me, he did you a favor."

"Then I guess I should give him the ring back."

"I say we hock it and fly to Vegas."

"I can't," Emmy said, actually wishing, if only for a moment, that she could.

Lindy was everything she wasn't. Petite, beautiful, wonderfully spontaneous. Emmy might have occasionally yearned to borrow Lindy's spur-of-the-moment, completely worry-free philosophy toward life, but the truth was if she hadn't been motivated to change for the man she'd intended to marry then she must be hopelessly set in her ways. "I have a new client," she said, feeling her world shift back into place again. "And it's a long way from Boston to Vegas. Hocking this ring will only get us halfway."

"True." Lindy gave the ring a look that couldn't have been more disdainful if she'd had a degree in gemology and a loupe up to her eye. "When you were describing Roger you should have substituted *cheap* for *boring.*" *Both times,* the tone of her voice said. "So what are you going to do? Besides work, I mean."

"I don't know. There's the hall, and the photographer—"

"And your list says you're getting married in three weeks, so… What? You're going to find some other guy? And if he's the same size as Roger, the tuxedo will fit him so that's one less detail that'll need to be dealt with?"

"Don't be ridiculous," Emmy said, "the tuxedo can be changed right up to the last minute."

Lindy laughed, which was what Emmy had intended. She'd been joking, of course. But there really should be something besides losing a deposit on the hall driving her to hang on to a fiancé who didn't want her. Love was the obvious reason, but she wasn't sure she believed in love—another saddlebag she was carrying around from her childhood. Not a lot of love floating around in the foster-care system. Mostly the people did it for the money. For herself, Emmy would settle for compatibility and affection. "How hard can it be to find another fiancé?"

"The guy at the end of the bar is kind of cute. You could slip something in his drink, or hide in an alley and coldcock the first likely man that comes along."

"I could hit you over the head and then I wouldn't have to finish this conversation."

Emmy waited, but there was no smart-aleck retort from Lindy. She'd frozen with her martini glass to her mouth, staring over the rim.

"Are you going to help me or not?"

"I found him." The glass thunked onto the tabletop, sloshing vermouth and gin over the rim.

Lindy tended to be a drama queen, but it had to be something earth-shattering for her to waste good alcohol, so Emmy turned around, peering through the midafternoon gloom of the hotel barroom. "The guy by the door? Tall, dark and disheveled?"

"He's yummy."

"He's messy." His hair looked like it had been attacked with a hacksaw, he sported a pair of worn-out jeans and a long-sleeved Henley shirt that had seen better days, and he needed a shave. "It's the middle of the afternoon on a workday and he's dressed like a bum."

"He could change his clothes, or better yet take them off entirely."

"He'd probably leave them on the floor."

"You're no fun."

Roger had accused her of that, too, Emmy recalled. It was harder to ignore the comment coming from her best friend, even though she knew Lindy wasn't serious.

Emmy had never pictured a man with his clothes off, but once she tried it she discovered some definite advantages— and not the ones she might have suspected. She hadn't considered herself a judgmental person either, but she realized she had a tendency to jump to conclusions about people based on what she saw on the outside. Once she ignored the packaging, all she saw was a tall man with dark hair, a five o'clock shadow, and a smile that lit up his entire face and threatened to spill over into the room. She knew that because he'd turned that smile on her, full wattage, and she definitely felt brighter. And warmer.

She mentally slapped the worn jeans and ratty shirt back on him before her temperature increased to a point where she risked setting off the overhead sprinklers. "Okay, maybe you have a point."

"And you didn't even have to make a list. Go talk to him."

"I have a client meeting me here…fifteen minutes ago."

"He's probably not coming. And since you have the next forty-five minutes dedicated to speaking with a man, why don't you see if this guy is willing to fill in?"

"My client is late, that's all." Not everyone had her sense of punctuality—hence the need for an efficiency expert. "He'll show up."

"Not before that guy does."

Sure enough, the man at the door was threading his way between the tables aiming, unmistakably, for theirs. And now that he was closer, Emmy could see his eyes. If his smile was trouble, his eyes were pure catastrophe, brown and warm and…interested. In her.

She grabbed Lindy's martini and downed what was left of it in one long gulp.

"Uh-oh. What was that for?"

"That was in case I do something stupid. Then when I wake up tomorrow morning I'll have something to blame it on."

"Sounds promising. Are you planning to wake up alone?"

"Yes." Absolutely. Not having anything to do with this man. When he got to the table she'd let Lindy do all the talking. But if he kept looking at her like that, there was no telling what would happen. Because when he looked at her like that she couldn't think of a single reason why she shouldn't ditch Lindy and her client and spend the rest of the day figuring out why this complete stranger knocked the lists right out of her head.

SHE WAS the wrong woman. Nick Porter knew that, even if he couldn't seem to keep his feet from carrying him in her direction. Sure, she had blond hair and blue eyes, which was the description he'd been given, but the blond hair was a head full of flyaway curls and the eyes were as blue as…something really, really blue.

There was more than one blond woman in the hotel bar, but this was the one Nick wanted to meet, which was convenient since he found himself standing beside her table. Unfortunately, his brain wasn't routing anything to his mouth so all he could do was stare at her, while she looked back at him with a quizzical, slightly amused expression on her face.

"Mr. Right?"

"What?" Nick glanced toward the sound of that voice, realizing for the first time there was another woman sitting at the table. The only response that came to mind was "you're in my seat," so he turned his attention back to the blonde and let the sight of her chase that rude comment out of his brain.

"That's my cue to leave," the second woman said. "I stand corrected, Emmy. It may be as easy to replace Roger as you think. And you get to trade up, too. Why did I ever doubt you?"

"The lists never fail," Emmy said.

"I don't think it's the list. I think it's testosterone."

Nick filtered their exchange through the impact the blonde's smile had on him, only picking up necessary information, such as her name. Emmy.

"Here, Mr…"

"Porter," he said absently, taking the chair the other woman vacated. "Nick Porter."

"Oh," Emmy said.

"You don't like my name?"

"Your name is fine. It just means you're my client." She watched her friend make her way to the door, and when she turned to him again, she'd traded in her resigned expression for one that was pleasantly blank. Businesslike. "I'm Emily Jones. Jones Consulting."

"Emmy," he corrected before the rest of her introduction battered its way through the brick wall of attraction he felt toward her. "You're the efficiency expert?"

"Yes."

"Are you sure?" he asked again, because he couldn't quite believe it. No self-respecting efficiency expert would go around looking so adorable. Efficiency experts carried clipboards and stopwatches and dressed in neat suits, not skirts and sweaters that tried for conservative without any real hope of pulling it off. They didn't slam back martinis, they nursed gin and tonics to make sure they didn't consume more than one ounce of alcohol per hour. And they were supposed to be all about work, not about driving every thought of it from a man's mind.

"I'm the efficiency expert," she insisted.

She was dishonesty in advertising is what she was, Nick decided. All that soft-looking blond hair and those big blue eyes, and she expected him to focus on business? But he took the hand she held out and immediately he was fine with that. "So you're the efficiency expert," he said. "Good." Now he didn't have to feel guilty for almost blowing off his meeting. Okay, so there wouldn't have been a whole lot of guilt, since one of his best friends from college—also known as his banker—had strong-armed him into this thing to begin with. It was that or no loan, and he really needed a loan.

The company he'd taken over from his father had been showing a little red ink lately, but it was just a temporary downturn in business. A loan would do the trick, Nick had decided, help Porter and Son last until the slow economy got back on its feet. Unfortunately, it wasn't as easy as that. He'd been turned down by nearly every bank in Boston. Except the bank where his friend worked, and even that approval came with a condition. Hire a consultant, get a turnaround plan and use the loan to put it into practice. Nick had no choice but to follow those instructions, at least until he got the damn loan. Then he'd put his own turnaround plan into place. He wasn't sure exactly what that plan might entail, but he knew that he was going to get his father's company back on track. And it wasn't going to take any efficiency expert to do it. All he needed was a great group of employees who'd been with the business for years, and some good old-fashioned hard work and determination....

He looked into Emmy Jones's sparkling eyes and forgot all about his plans and his objections and his need to dig deep and find some determination inside himself before it was too late. He forgot about his banker/friend and his employees and the weight of his father's legacy. When he looked at Emmy Jones his mind went on vacation and the rest of him was left to run the show. Not good. He'd come here to get rid of the efficiency expert; kissing her wouldn't exactly accomplish that goal. And he wanted, badly, to kiss her. At least for starters.

"Why don't we go over the contract?" she suggested.

Nope, Nick didn't want to do that, but they had to talk about something or he was going to do something they'd both regret—all right, he wouldn't regret it, but he'd probably get slapped. "Who's Roger and why do you have to replace him?" he asked, seizing on the first thing that popped into his head that didn't have anything to do with his job. Or hers.

"Roger was my fiancé."

"Was?"

"He backed out of our wedding."

"So you came here to replace him?" Nick asked, not wasting his time on sympathy since she didn't sound too upset. "Maybe you should play the field a little before you jump into another serious relationship. I could help you with that."

"Lindy was only joking," she said. "And even if she wasn't, you're a client and I never mix business and personal. And you were late."

"Late would have been after the wedding."

She frowned at him and even that was cute. Odd, Nick thought, that he should have this strong a reaction to a woman he'd only just met, but the more she tried to set a professional tone for their conversation the more determined he was to get some sort of personal response from her.

"I'm sorry I was late," he said, realizing belatedly that he should probably apologize. "Time kind of got away from me."

She reached across the table, and took his hand—not to mention his breath. She pushed his sleeve up and brushed her fingers across the back of his wrist. Little black spots danced in front of his eyes.

"Buy a watch," she said.

"Huh?" he croaked.

"You're not wearing a watch. It's hard to be on time if you don't actually know what time it is."

Nick pulled his arm back. "How do you know it's not on my other wrist?" And how was she not affected by touching him?

"You're right-handed, which means you wear your watch on your left wrist."

She sounded calm and efficient. But she wasn't meeting his eyes anymore. Further investigation revealed the pulse pounding wildly in the hollow of her throat. His ego did a few cartwheels. Until he reminded himself that she was clearly a woman who made a decision and stuck to it. And she'd decided not to be interested in him that way.

So he'd have to change her mind.

"About your business, Mr. Porter..."

"We're not going to have any fun at all if you don't call me Nick."

There she went, frowning again, as though she didn't know what fun was or how to have it. Maybe she didn't resemble an efficiency expert on the outside, but she definitely had the inner workings of one. "Look, Emmy, I'm a pretty laid-back guy most of the time. But my dad left me that business, and I...promised him I'd keep it going. It was suggested that I hire an efficiency expert, and you came highly recommended." By a guy who held Nick's fate in the palm of his hand. In truth, she'd been foisted on him, Nick decided, because foisting was what happened to you when you had no choice. Nick decided to keep that to himself, though, verbally and, he hoped, expression-wise. It wasn't much of a challenge, since having Emmy foisted upon him didn't feel like such a hardship.

She studied his face for a moment, then, apparently convinced of his sincerity, she opened a ruthlessly organized briefcase and extracted two copies of the contract they'd drawn up and traded via fax. "'Streamline assembly operations,'" she read. "'Redesign workflow, organize the office.' That's what we agreed on, correct?"

Nick chewed on all that for a moment. To a man who didn't so much as plan his next meal in advance, Emmy's sense of order was astounding. And just a little scary.

Scary or not, his decision had already been made. He pulled the contract over in front of him, searched his breast pocket and came up empty—probably because there wasn't any pocket. After a brief and futile internal debate he plucked the pen out of her hand.

She watched him calmly, and when he slid the paperwork back to her she looked at the illegible scrawl that passed for his signature beneath her precisely written name. "Here's your copy," she said, returning one of the signed contracts to him, "and this one is for my files," and back it went into her briefcase.

Nick rubbed his damp palms on his thighs and put the contract out of his mind, and so what if it felt as if he was hiring her under false pretenses? They were both getting something out of the deal—his loan, her consulting fee. And more importantly he got to see her again, because as little as he was looking forward to having an efficiency expert underfoot at Porter and Son, having Emmy Jones under... No, he probably shouldn't finish that thought, or the mental picture that went along with it. As it was, it would be hard enough to face her on Monday morning. In more ways than one.

Chapter Two

Promptly at 8:00 a.m. the following Monday Emmy pushed through the door of Porter and Son, Inc., Practical Jokes and Everyday Gags, and presented herself at the desk of the receptionist. Her name plate said Stella, the expression on her face said she sampled the company's products on a regular basis and found them highly entertaining, and she was eager to help, which she displayed by saying, "Can I help you?" and folding her hands together as if she were praying Emmy would say yes.

She was so bubbly Emmy took an involuntary step backward, worried the woman might overflow cheerfulness all over her new gray suit. "I'm here to see Nick Porter," she said, and she handed over a business card—which was where the day began to go south.

Emmy knew her day had just headed south because this was the point at which her first day on a new job always began to go south. The instant they found out who she was.

Stella read the card, then turned it over as if she expected to see a smiley face on the back. And when she didn't find a "just kidding," or a disclaimer, or a mitigating explanation of any kind, she looked up at Emmy, mouth agape, eyes wide and filled with horrified fascination, not quite believing anyone was brazen enough to walk bald-faced into a perfectly respectable place of business with a card that read—

"Efficiency Expert," Stella said, her personality morphing from bubbly to…another word that started with *b*. "Mr. Porter isn't here."

Emmy consulted her watch. Eight-oh-five. No surprise there. "I'll wait," she said, hoping Nick would make an appearance soon. Stella looked as though she was sucking on a pickle, and she'd already proven herself the kind of woman who didn't come equipped with a filter between her feelings and the rest of the world.

"It could be some time before Mr. Porter shows—uh, arrives," Stella said, frowning when Emmy appropriated one of the faux-leather lobby chairs for her briefcase and the other for her backside. "In fact, I'm almost sure Mr. Porter is out of the city this morning. Far out of the city. Visiting our rubber supplier."

Emmy lifted her eyes from the paperwork she'd pulled out of her briefcase. "Rubber supplier?"

"Whoopee cushions, balloons, paddle balls. Rubber. What did you think I was talking about?"

A joke that took nine months to get to the punch line. "Nothing," Emmy said.

"Perhaps you'd like to come back another time. Or better yet, you could call and speak with Mr. Porter. If he's interested, he'll set up an appointment."

Yeah, like that call would go through. "We have—we *had*—an eight o'clock appointment today."

A fact he obviously hadn't shared with his secretary, and if he wasn't going to tell anyone why he'd hired an efficiency expert, then neither was Emmy. There was no point in trying to ingratiate herself, anyway. No matter what she did, it wouldn't put a dent in the hostility factor. Employees generally took an immediate dislike to efficiency experts, thinking they came equipped with pink slips and a one-track mind when it came to prettying up a company's bottom line.

In the current climate of corporate downsizing Emmy could understand the paranoia, but her job was to make the company run more efficiently. It was up to management to decide how to deal with the results. To her mind, the best way to use up the extra capacity that came along with running more efficiently was to increase sales. Unfortunately that took time, and most owners chose to trim payroll until they reached a point where increased sales demanded additional help. And wasn't it convenient to have an efficiency expert right there to blame?

Nick Porter didn't seem like that kind of guy, although Emmy had no idea how in the world she'd come up with that assessment of his character after a half-hour-long meeting that had started off strange and grown stranger. Toward the end of it she'd begun to wonder exactly why he'd hired her. At best he'd seemed ambivalent about signing the contract. On the other hand he'd seemed a little too eager to have her around—and not in a professional capacity. He definitely hadn't looked at her like a man who was hiring a consultant.

She must have lost her mind—she *had* lost her mind—but she'd really liked the way he'd looked at her.

"He has a girlfriend."

Emmy wiped the dreamy smile off her face, adding *way too observant* to Stella's list of character traits, and *crazy* to her own.

She had no business thinking about Nick like that when she was still dealing with the aftermath of Roger— Okay, she allowed, that was a bit of an overstatement. She hadn't thought of Roger more than once or twice in the last couple of days, and she couldn't say she was all that broken up. It was more of an irritation, actually. Her real problem was the wedding guests. She didn't know what to tell them. She'd thought about that a lot—until it occurred to her that almost all of them were from Roger's side, and he could deal with his own friends and relatives.

That harmless bit of retribution felt so good she'd decided to take it another step, namely the wedding itself. She'd made all the arrangements for the ceremony and reception, and since Roger was the one who'd backed out, and the deposit checks had been written against his bank account anyway, he could unarrange it all. And since she was going to dump that unpleasant task on him, the truth was Roger didn't really leave much of an aftermath.

But she had learned something from him. Stay away from men. She could barely form lasting friendships with women. What made her think she could have an actual long-term relationship with a man? Men were a whole other species.

Not that it was going to be an issue, because she'd already decided to keep her interaction with Nick Porter on a strictly business level. Polite but firm, that was the ticket. Cool and competent and professional. And the next time he looked at her like she was the only woman in the world, or smiled at her like she was the fulfillment of all his fantasies, she was going to tell him—

Nick walked through one of the two doorways beyond Stella's desk, stopped in front of Emmy, and looked at her with that unnerving intensity. She couldn't have finished her thought with paste-on letters and explicit instructions.

"Good, you're here," he said, and when she simply sat there, he gathered her papers and briefcase, took her by the elbow, and ushered her through the other door behind Stella's desk. It led to his office, and he talked the whole way. "Tripod went missing this morning. He's my next-door neighbor's dog and he only has three legs—the dog, I mean. My neighbor has the usual two."

He paused expectantly, but Emmy was speechless, and it had nothing to do with the combined leg count of Nick's neighbor and his dog. She'd forgotten how darned handsome he was. And how warm she felt when he smiled at her.

"Anyway," he continued, "by the time Tripod turned up I was blocked in because the Martins across the street were getting new dining-room furniture, and I didn't have the heart to make them move the truck. They've been waiting forever for that furniture, so I figured it would be faster to help them unload it instead. And then I had to take another shower."

And the truly amazing part, at least to Emmy's mind, was that Nick knew the names of all his neighbors, and their pets *and* their furniture-buying habits. Nor was it confined to his neighbors.

"When I finally got here I realized Marty Henshaw was late—probably trouble with his car again—so line one was down, and I filled in for a half hour." He sniffed at his armpit. "Do you think I need another shower?"

"No, you smell pretty…" she said before she could stop herself. "Uh, you're fine."

"Pretty fine," Nick said. "I'll take that."

Okay, don't look at him, Emmy lectured herself. Eye contact with Nick Porter wasn't in her best interest. Concentrating on work was. "This person who was late—"

"Marty Henshaw. Gosh you look pretty this morning."

Emmy tried to hold it together, but a sigh slipped out. This situation called for drastic action. She took a sheet of paper from her briefcase and handed it to him. "This is a basic questionnaire, Mr. Porter—"

"Nick." He brushed a curl off her forehead, his finger grazing her skin.

She began to tremble. And panic. "We have to get a couple of things straight. I'm here to do a job. There'll be no more compliments and no more touching. And no more smiling."

He wiped the smile off his face, but the corners of his mouth twitched suspiciously. Emmy got the distinct impression he wasn't taking her seriously.

"How about after hours?" he asked. "Can I smile then?"

"After hours you can smile at anybody you want. But it won't be me."

That did it. The smile was gone completely. Emmy missed it. "I'm sorry, that was rude."

His eyes began to warm up.

"But I meant it," she said. "We have to keep business and…"

"Pleasure separate? No problem."

"No pleasure," she said firmly, adding *watch my words* to her mental list of rules governing how to deal with Nick Porter. "There's only going to be business."

"Why?"

"Because."

"That's not an answer."

"It's the only one I have. I don't want to get involved in anything personal, and since my reasons are, well, personal," not to mention confusing, even to her, "I'm not getting into them."

"It's Roger, isn't it?"

No. Definitely not Roger. But if she said that, Nick would want to know the real reason. Emmy didn't know the real reason, but she knew there was fear involved. A lot of fear. And if something about Nick Porter scared her that much, it could only be in her best interest to keep her distance. "I'm madly in love with Roger, and he broke my heart," she said. "It wouldn't be fair to get involved with anyone else."

"Nope. That's not it."

"Yes, it is."

"You only think it's because of Roger, but really it's because of me."

"Because of you?"

"I'm irresistible."

Emmy knew it would only encourage him, but she couldn't help laughing.

"It's true," he insisted. "Look at me."

He spread his hands and she followed directions. It wasn't eye contact, but it wasn't any less dangerous. He was attractive, no doubt about it, and he was tall which, being tall herself, Emmy considered a definite plus. And he obviously kept in shape; he wasn't exactly dressed for the executive suite, but if he looked that good in Dockers, he'd be killer in a suit. And she'd be dead meat.

But it wasn't just his face and body. Nick Porter had that thing, that indefinable quality that made actors movie stars and pretty girls supermodels. You just wanted to be around him, Emmy concluded, and talk to him and look at him. It didn't make any sense, but that was why they called it the X-factor. There weren't any words descriptive enough to give it an actual name.

"I'm entertaining, too," he said, taking her long perusal and the resulting silence as agreement. "I'm funny and dependable—"

"No, you're not. We've only met twice and you've been late both times."

"You're right, I just said that because I thought it would appeal to an efficiency expert. But punctuality is highly overrated. There's more to life than work."

"I know." She just didn't like any of the other parts. "But work is what we're supposed to be doing right now. Besides, you have a girlfriend, and I doubt she'd appreciate your efforts to appeal to me."

"Let me guess, Stella told you that. She thinks every woman I meet is after my money."

"You don't have any money. Your business is in debt."

"I know. That's why you're here. Who would've thought being broke would turn into such an advantage? Although I have to admit I'm not actually broke. I have a trust fund."

"So women *are* after your money."

"Sometimes. But the important thing is *you're* not, and since I'm not currently dating anyone except you—"

"We're not dating."

"Yet. We will be. Eventually I'll wear you down, and before you know it you'll be introducing me to your parents. Once I meet your mom you're toast. Moms love me."

Emmy didn't say anything, but she made sure her expression was blank. She didn't exactly dwell on her childhood, or the foster homes, but she didn't have any trouble with the memories, either. Her parents—her mother especially—was the one area of her past she couldn't bear to think about. It hurt too much.

"I said something wrong."

"My parents are dead." It looked as though he might reach for her, so Emmy eased away from him. "It happened a long time ago. I barely remember them, and it's personal. I'm here to talk about your business. Do you want to save it?"

For a minute she didn't think he was going to respect her boundaries—or agree with her. But then he nodded and she was able to relax. As much, she figured, as she'd ever be able to relax around Nick.

"Good, then let's get started."

Chapter Three

Emmy spent the rest of the day observing Nick's employees. Nick spent the rest of the day observing Emmy. The employees didn't care much for being observed. Emmy was oblivious to everything but work. Nick had the time of his life.

She was so cute with her clipboard and stopwatch, brow furrowed in concentration, tucking her flyaway blond hair behind her ear every other minute. That hair gave him real hope where she was concerned. If she'd been as no-nonsense as she claimed to be, she'd have tamed her hair back into some kind of ugly, efficient bun. Nick couldn't think of anything worse than that, so it was a relief that she was still wandering around with a head full of wild Shirley Temple curls.

And she was surprisingly good with people—or she would have been if she'd let them in. She asked questions, and she listened so intently to the answers that whoever she was speaking with couldn't help but be flattered despite themselves. But every time talk strayed to the personal, she shut down, the person on the other side of the conversation backed off, and Emmy moved on to the next work station, personal involvement rolling off her as though she walked around in a Teflon isolation bubble. She'd done the same thing when he mentioned her mother, Nick remembered, only the bubble hadn't been made of Teflon, it had been made of sadness.

Well, he was just the guy to burst her bubble—and where the heck had that thought come from? Nick wondered. Being attracted to her was one thing, anything else was moving way too fast, and Nick made it a point never to move too fast.

Yet there was something about Emmy Jones. Part of it was knowing she'd lost her parents at a young age. Nick could sympathize; his mother had died before he was twelve years old, and he remembered that time with perfectly awful clarity. There was something more drawing him to Emmy, though, a level of curiosity and fascination that pushed him beyond his normal take-it-as-it-comes approach to romance. He was so anxious to see her that he was actually on time the next morning, waiting in the parking lot for her. Emmy was late.

"There you are," he said when she finally pulled up and was climbing out of her car. "I guess I can call off the St. Bernards."

"Are those the dogs that carry little kegs around their necks? Because I could use a drink about now."

And he could use a cold shower. She reached into the front seat to gather her purse and briefcase, her skirt hiked up high enough to show about a mile of leg, and Nick could practically feel brain cells dying from lack of oxygen. Fortunately he didn't care because most of his attention was focused way south of his brain.

"Considering how my day started, it's probably best if I don't remember any of it," she mumbled from the car's interior.

She straightened, but Nick's brain was slow to keep up. "There are other ways to forget."

"I've tried ice cream already."

"For breakfast?"

"Trust me, this was the kind of unforeseen event that called for drastic measures. But Roger is too much for even triple chocolate fudge to banish."

Nick tore his eyes off her legs and checked back in to the conversation. "Roger, as in the guy who dumped you? What did he want?"

She walked around him and headed for the building. "He wanted to get his things."

"And you couldn't tear yourself away?"

"I had to stick around and guard my furniture. It turns out Roger has a pretty inventive memory when it comes to what he brought with him when he moved in."

"I could talk to him for you." Or punch him.

She took in the expression on his face and the curl to his fingers. "I don't think it's a good idea for you and Roger to interact."

"Funny, I'm having the same thought where you're concerned."

Emmy rolled her eyes. Nick would have been insulted if she didn't look so adorable doing it.

"Here's the report I wrote up last night," she said, "some preliminary observations about the way your business runs, and some areas we can study for possible efficiency improvements."

Nick took the neat manila folder she handed him and completely ignored it. There was some serious heat jumping around inside him, and he had two choices, punch Roger or kiss Emmy. He took one look and decided punching Roger wasn't going to cool him off. Kissing Emmy wasn't going to cool him off, either, but at least he wouldn't hurt his hand.

For the moment, though, she was only interested in work so he had to humor her. And control himself.

She didn't make it easy.

When they got to Nick's office, Emmy took the file folder from him and set it on the desk. "Point one. Starting and quitting times have to be enforced," she read, still standing so Nick had no choice but to follow along over her shoulder. He stood as close as he thought he could get away with, but not so close that his brain checked out. "Do you think that's realistic?"

She brushed the back of her neck where his breath had washed over her skin, then she moved away. Nick let her because he'd seen the list. It was long. Plenty of time and opportunity to be close to her.

"Every other company in the world seems to find it perfectly acceptable to ask their employees to come in at a specific time," she said.

"I've known most of these people since I was a kid. They're more like aunts and uncles and cousins than employees."

"Okay, but if you go out of business all your relatives will wind up in the unemployment line."

"You've got a point." And since her suggestion was basically harmless, it wouldn't hurt to play along. "I guess I could talk to them about getting to work on time. But people have problems. School buses are late, babysitters are sick, ex-fiancés come back to steal furniture."

For a second Nick thought she was going to smile. She pressed her lips together and tapped the paper instead. That was an invitation if ever he'd seen one, so he moved in behind her again.

"Point two," he read. "Cross-training." Cross-training was a pretty self-explanatory concept, but Nick let her talk so he could watch her.

"You should make sure your employees are trained on each other's jobs," she said. "That way if someone is late or sick, another employee can fill in, and you can rotate the employees to keep the line running. You won't get full production, but you won't be dead in the water either."

She kept talking. Nick nodded and made understanding

noises so it seemed like he·was following along, but he'd given up listening for watching. Efficiency was a necessary evil for him, but he loved the way Emmy's eyes lit up when she got into the subject. And she was really getting into it, moving around, gesturing, pushing her hair off her face. He loved it when she did that. And he loved the trim little suit she was wearing. He loved it that she was tall and passionate. All her passion was channeled into her work, but he could expand on that.

"Point seven," she said, "find a way to get Nick to concentrate on business while he still owns one."

"Uh-huh," he said, nodding and smiling. She came over to stand in front of him and he just naturally stood a bit straighter. Okay, so he liked her tallness, as long as he was taller. He was old-fashioned about that sort of thing.

"You're not listening to me," she said.

"Yes, I am."

"Tell me what I just said."

Nick racked his brain for all of two seconds and then he grinned. "You said you'd love to go out to dinner with me tonight."

"I don't have time for dinner."

"You're an efficiency expert. Don't you sit down promptly at 8:00 p.m. and eat all the food groups balanced in accordance with the current FDA nutritional pyramid?"

"And I schedule exactly 23.6 minutes every evening so I can chew each bite forty times. Unfortunately that means I don't have time for restaurants and meaningful conversation."

Translation, she didn't have time for Nick.

She tucked her list of observations back into the manila folder and handed it to him. "If it's any consolation, I will go out with you now, to your factory floor."

He shrugged. "It's a start."

The factory was a cavernous, well-lit space, big roll-up doors open to the let in the warm spring cross-breeze. Yesterday it had been decorated in industrial chic—safety posters, calendars, gray lockers, fake-wood-grain tables and metal chairs in the lunch room. Today it was decorated in Emmy Jones. Pictures of her hung everywhere, on the walls, from the rafters, on the fridge in the break room, on the sides of the conveyors. A couple of Nick's employees even had them taped to their backs, and all of the pictures had big red targets over her face. As soon as she stepped around Nick, and the employees caught sight of her, she was greeted with a ragged chorus of whoopee-cushion raspberries.

"I'm sorry," Nick said to Emmy.

"No need to apologize. This is normal."

"It's normal for people who want you dead."

"They don't want me dead. They're just comfortable with the way things are. Once they understand that I'm here to make their jobs more secure, they'll stop hating me." She laid a hand on his arm. "Trust me, this is nothing compared to some of the things that have been done to me."

Even if she hadn't been touching him voluntarily, her words would have stopped Nick. The idea of anybody doing anything mean to Emmy got his hackles up. It was a new experience for him. Except for wanting to pound Roger. "Like what?"

"Lots of stuff has happened to my car. My tires were glued to the parking lot once, and when I worked at the forklift company it was—"

"Up in the air."

"Forty feet. They made really big forklifts." She smiled and shook her head. "It's been filled with packing peanuts and shrink-wrapped."

Nick laughed. "Pretty inventive."

"So are these guys," Emmy said. "They got pictures of me from somewhere."

"Camera phone probably."

"That explains all the wonderful poses. I particularly like the one where my mouth is open and one eye is shut. I look drunk."

"You look beautiful."

"That's because the bull's-eye hides most of my face."

"Nope, that's not it. I can see your face just fine." And he kind of liked the target. It summed up his intentions; he had her in the crosshairs and she wasn't getting away. He might not be the most focused or driven guy in the world, but when he went after something he wanted, he generally got it. And he wanted Emmy Jones.

WHEN Emmy's doorbell rang that evening, she checked her watch. She already knew what time it was. She always knew what time it was. She checked her watch because she wasn't expecting anyone, and no one ever called on her unexpectedly, not at seven fifty-eight in the evening. She looked out her peephole and saw Nick Porter. Mystery solved.

Nick Porter didn't know the meaning of appointments or calling ahead or work versus personal. Nick Porter didn't know the meaning of the word *no*. She could leave him standing out there until he figured it out, or she could open the door and explain it to him. She opted for the second choice, because she didn't want him loitering on her doorstep all night—she didn't have any doubt he'd understand why she refused to let him in, but he'd be too stubborn to go away.

"Go away," she said as soon as she opened the door.

He didn't say anything. In fact, he stared at her for so long she became self-conscious, adjusting her hooded sweatshirt, feeling her sweatpants for holes in strategic places. And when she didn't find any she got freaked out. "What's wrong with you?"

"It's not me, it's you."

She covered her mouth. "Something in my teeth?" Or her nose! She moved her fingers northward, talking through them. "Be specific."

"You're not wearing a suit."

"Okay." Weird. "But I'm completely clothed, and I'm not working—that is, I'm working at home." If he thought she wasn't busy he'd never leave. "I change my clothes when I get home from work, just like normal people."

"I miss your legs," he said, easing her aside and stepping into her entryway. "I like looking at them."

And she liked that he liked them. Bad, very bad. "They're still there, under the sweatpants. I was going to exercise. Yoga."

"That explains the great legs," Nick said. "I'll bet you're really flexible, too."

"Not so much. I'm just a beginner. I used to do aerobics, but lately I've been kind of…restless. I thought maybe yoga would have a calming effect." And why she felt a need to explain that to him she had no idea. Nervous rambling, that was it. He was looking at her in that intent way he had, and she was letting her mouth run because it was better to babble than throw herself into his arms, which was what she really wanted to do.

"Go ahead, don't mind me."

"What? Oh, yoga." Right, Emmy thought, like she was going to do Downward-Facing Dog with him around. Getting sweaty didn't hold any appeal, either, at least not getting sweaty alone. "I think you should leave." She held the door open, but he stuffed his hands in his pockets and grinned. And she gave up. "How'd you get my home address?"

"Your friend, Lindy. She called looking for you. She

wanted to know if you were available tonight, but I told her you already had a date with me."

"We don't have a date."

"Sure we do. I asked you this morning, and you didn't say no."

"I'm saying it now."

"But you don't mean it."

"Yes, I do." At least she wanted to. And once he left she'd be relieved. "We have a working relationship, Nick. That's all."

Nick studied her for a long, uncomfortable moment, his expression, for once, inscrutable. When he pulled the door open, she thought he'd finally gotten the message. But he didn't walk out. Instead, he crowded her back behind the door, blocking her in with his body.

She should have felt threatened. She was scared to death, but not of being hurt by him. At least not physically. "You really need to go home."

"I will." Instead of backing off, though, he leaned forward.

Emmy leaned away. "You can't just show up at my house and—"

"I'm spontaneous," he whispered, his lips a breath away from hers. "It's part of my appeal."

Of all the things that appealed to her about Nick Porter, spontaneity was pretty much last on the list. She liked things budgeted, itemized, organized and timed down to the last second. Nick Porter was an undisciplined, disorganized wild card. Nick Porter blew her schedules right out of the water, and threatened to drown her self-control. She had the insane urge to fist her hands in his shirt and drag him against her, lips and all.

She planted both hands on his chest and locked her elbows instead. Her palms began to tingle, and the tingle spread all the way to the crown of her head and the ends of her toes, lingering at all the obvious places in between. And it didn't stop at a tingle. There was heat, too. Emmy pushed him away before the heat and tingle could gang up on her self-control and make her do something that she'd regret.

Nick stared at her for a second, looking as shell-shocked as she felt. "I'm going to kiss you, Emmy," he said, adding, "not tonight," when she stepped up the pressure against his chest. "I'm going to kiss you when you least expect it. And you won't push me away." Then he walked out the door. He bounced off the doorjamb first, but eventually he made it outside and wobbled off toward the street.

Emmy didn't find her voice until he was long gone and she heard someone shouting at her.

"Emmy? Are you there? Emmy?"

She stared at the phone in her hand, wondering how it had gotten there and when she'd dialed. "Lindy?"

"Emmy. What's going on? Are you all right?"

"No. Why did you give Nick Porter my address?"

"So that's why I hear panic in your voice. I thought that would be your reaction to him."

"Then why—"

"Because you can use his kind of panic."

And that was why Emmy heard smugness in Lindy's voice. "He tried to kiss me."

"Tried?"

"I almost let him."

"Why didn't you, Emmy? I think this guy is *the* guy for you. Your soul mate."

"You don't believe in soul mates."

"For me. I think they're fine for everyone else. And even if Nick Porter isn't your soul mate, it's about time you had some fun. You deserve it after Roger."

"Fun is highly overrated. You have fun all the time, Lindy, and frankly you don't seem completely satisfied with your life."

"Oooh, the claws are out." Lindy laughed, but there was a note of strain beneath the amusement.

"I'm sorry," Emmy said. "That was mean."

"It was also true, but we're not talking about me. You're afraid of Nick Porter, and you have good reason to be."

"What good reason?"

"You're going to have to figure that out for yourself."

"Thanks, Lindy. Someday I'll return the favor."

She broke the connection, but she wasn't really angry with Lindy. Because Lindy was right. Nick Porter scared Emmy. A lot. And it wasn't as much of a mystery as she claimed. She liked the way he looked at her and the way he smiled at her, as if she were special. She'd never been special to anyone but Lindy—not to a man, anyway. Definitely not to Roger. Roger had left her each morning with a dry peck on the lips and a list of tasks he expected her to perform. Pick up the dry cleaning, reschedule his dental appointment, and wouldn't it be nice to have meat loaf for dinner.

When Nick smiled at her, she could tell she was the only item on his list, and he didn't want anything from her. Okay, he wanted something. The problem was she wanted it too. But she couldn't have it. Getting involved with Nick would be a mistake for too many reasons to itemize.

She popped the yoga video out of the VCR and put in the most frenetic aerobics tape she could find. As tense as she was, it would take the Dalai Lama himself to meditate her into a state where she had any hope of sleep. Since she doubted he'd come down from his mountain to help her work off a case of hormonal overload, a couple of hours of exhausting exercise might do the trick. Or it might not. Maybe the only thing that could help her work off this much tension was the man who'd caused it.

Nick Porter, however, was the one remedy she didn't dare try.

Chapter Four

Most of the week passed in a blur. Emmy spent it hunched over her clipboard, nose to the grindstone, observing Nick's employees and ignoring their commentary. Nick spent it behaving himself. Their paths crossed every now and again, but he made himself scarce to the point that when Friday afternoon arrived, and her weekly progress report was due, she had to go in search of him.

For the first time in her life, Emmy saw the advantage in procrastination. There really wasn't any progress to report, she told herself, unless she counted the rise in the hostility level. She'd worn jeans and an oxford shirt, hoping she'd fit in better. The only way she'd attract more attention was if she'd decided to show up naked.

She'd ditched her clipboard in favor of her briefcase, laying it open on the high table where the shipping clerk signed in raw material and checked out finished goods. She ought to at least pretend to be busy, she decided, maybe take notes or something. So she retrieved a pen and pad of paper from her case and meandered aimlessly, stopping to lean one hip against a pallet of boxes, watching the activity and letting her mind wander. The employees were bustling around, pausing every now and again to shoot her fulminating glares. They didn't bother her. What bothered her was Nick, and not in the way she'd expected.

The last four days had been all about business. The few times she and Nick had interacted, he hadn't mentioned the night at her house. Neither had she. He wasn't making passes, he wasn't trying to kiss her, or touch her hair or anything. He even listened politely to what she had to say about the company, although he didn't do anything to implement change, and his employees had only become more sullen and resistant. But at least he was listening.

Emmy was the one whose mind kept wandering.

"Emmy."

She jumped, spinning around, one hand plastered over her suddenly pounding heart. Nick was standing a bit behind and to one side of her, just out of her peripheral vision before she'd turned around. The sight of him didn't do a lot to calm her down, the upheaval just affected different parts of her. "How long have you been there?" she asked when she could manage to string words together and make them sound normal.

He shrugged, smile polite, eyes distant. "Couple of minutes."

No wonder the death glares she'd been getting from the employees were worse than usual.

"Penny for your thoughts," he said.

She turned and set the pad on top of the pallet. Bad idea.

Nick came over to stand beside her. He wasn't touching her, or looking at her, or smiling, but the parts of her that hadn't gone all soft and melty were tensed so tightly she was on the verge of a head-to-toe charley horse. Not that she was complaining, because the tense parts of her were keeping the other parts from jumping him.

His comment about kissing her when she least expected it

was getting to her. Not only was she expecting it constantly, she was on the verge of kissing him so she could get it over with before she went completely insane. Okay, that wasn't the only reason she wanted to kiss him. The more she thought about it...

And that was exactly what he wanted. Her thinking about it, wondering, giving in to the inevitable. He had no idea just how stubborn she could be.

She blinked a couple of times to get her eyes to focus, unlocked her jaw and opened the file. "R-raw materials," she stuttered out, her body slower to get with the program.

Nick moved closer, still not touching her. But she could tell he was amused. And smug.

It was that last reaction that put the steel into her backbone. "I'll need a list of your raw materials, where they come from, how they're ordered, how much at a time and how they're delivered." She made the mistake of looking up at him. Eye contact had always been big with Emmy, but she forgot that eye contact with Nick was dangerous to her self-control.

Nick wasn't immune, either. "Emmy..." he said, leaning in, voice low, all his employees stopping what they were doing to gawk like commuters at a traffic accident.

"You'll need to increase sales," Emmy continued, writing down Increase Sales next to 1 on her pad. "Either spend more time yourself or hire someone to focus exclusively on selling."

"Can't afford that," Nick said, frowning but not moving off.

Emmy cut her eyes to their audience, and Nick got the idea. More importantly, he took a step back.

"If you don't want to increase your payroll, you could send out a mailing," Emmy said. "Or you could do it yourself. Face-to-face is best anyway, and you're so personable and persuasive, all you have to do is waltz in with that face and that smile—"

Nick grinned wider with each compliment.

"—and you shouldn't have any trouble increasing your sales," Emmy finished. "Especially if you're selling to a woman."

The grin only got wider. "Is that jealousy I'm hearing?"

Emmy caught herself on the verge of denial, and shrugged instead. "If it increases your sales, do whatever you're comfortable with."

"So if I wanted to flirt with them?"

She looked him straight in the eye, and so what if she didn't like the thought of him flirting with other women. "No harm in that."

"What if I take them out to lunch?"

"Lots of people do business lunches."

"And dinner?" He eased toward her, crowding her back between the pallet of boxes she'd been leaning against and another about two feet away.

She held her ground—okay, there was a wall behind her, but refusing to back off was more of a statement that she could resist his charm. So what if he'd come so close she was practically nose-to-chin with him, and she caught herself thinking about how easy it would be to raise up onto her toes, lay her mouth on his and put herself out of her misery? She looked around but the place was devoid of workers, break-time being more attractive than spying on the boss and his loathsome efficiency expert.

"And business dinners," she said, telling herself to get a grip. "And sporting events, and concerts, although those are kind of expensive undertakings with your current budget constraints."

"What if we had dinner at my house?"

Her gaze shot to his, but she was seeing him in candlelight, with another woman. Mere feet from his bedroom. "Do you always have trouble drawing a line between business and personal?"

"I was trying to get a rise out of you," he said.

"I know." And she'd been trying to deflate him. They'd both been successful. She was still struggling with resentments toward strange and completely innocent women, and for once Nick looked something other than laid-back and foolishly happy with life. He looked angry.

Emmy started forward. He stepped in front of her, trapping her in the narrow aisle. She couldn't go around him, and she couldn't get by him. She wanted to keep right on going until she ended up against that nice, firm chest she remembered— or at least her palms remembered, judging by the way they were tingling. And the tingle was spreading so fast she was in danger of becoming one big mess of quivering nerve endings.

There's a remedy for that, a little voice whispered, a little voice she wouldn't shush because she was a realist. She wanted him to kiss her, there was no getting around it. But you didn't always get what you wanted, and even if you did, what you wanted wasn't always good for you. She'd learned that a long time ago. Apparently, what she hadn't learned was how to hide her feelings.

"You want me to kiss you," Nick said.

"No. Absolutely not. No way."

"All week you've been waiting for me to try to kiss you, but I haven't and you're disappointed."

"I am not disappointed," she said with absolute conviction because what she was was ticked off. Maybe when she got past that she'd have room for disappointment, but at the moment she was riding high on outrage and pure unadulterated lust. Who did he think he was anyway, getting her all stirred up and then not coming through? "I don't want you to kiss me."

"But you want me to try."

She huffed out a breath and crossed her arms. Yeah, absolutely she wanted him to try. But that was only ego. And libido. And she certainly wasn't telling him that.

"You don't want me to try?"

Emmy stayed mum, but the reason she didn't have an answer was because Nick sounded so...hurt. And she felt guilty. Even though she hadn't exactly welcomed his attentions, outright rejection just seemed cruel.

"Nick—" Emmy began.

This time Stella saved her from saying something she'd regret, which was probably the last thing Stella would have wanted to do. Emmy caught movement out of the corner of her eye, and when she turned around there Stella was, standing by the shipping counter where Emmy had left her briefcase.

"Can I help you?" Emmy asked her.

Stella's hands shot to her hips, and her eyes narrowed. Clearly she wasn't happy, and she wasn't talking to Emmy. "You have a phone call, Mr. Porter," she said to Nick.

"Take a message."

Stella downgraded her expression to sour-pickle. Emmy considered throwing herself into Nick's arms just to see how cranky Stella could get, but she'd probably give the woman a stroke. And she probably wouldn't be able to stop at just being in Nick's arms. And Nick would definitely misconstrue her motives.

Stella scuttled back into the office. Emmy took advantage of Nick's distraction, slipping by him and walking over to check out her briefcase. She didn't know what Stella had hoped to find, but there were no big secrets in there, no clandestine meetings, no international spying. No secret plans outlining her designs on Nick. Just the file containing the progress report, lying half on top of her day planner, which was still open to that day, work at Nick's, dinner with Lindy.

"What were you going to say?" Nick asked, coming over to join her and craning his neck to see over her shoulder.

Emmy snapped her day planner shut. "Nothing I haven't said before, and you didn't listen any of the other times."

"I listened. I didn't believe you."

And in case she didn't get the message, he was crowding her again. Emmy refused to back off. She was a mess of physical and emotional agitation, the scant inch of air between them was scorching with heat and humming with tension, but retreat would be the same as admitting he was getting to her, and that would be as good as telling him he was right to keep pushing.

"If you really want me to give up, I will," Nick said.

Emmy handed him her progress report, shut her briefcase and headed for the big door that led out to the parking lot and her getaway vehicle.

"Fine, just walk away," Nick snapped at her.

Emmy couldn't resist a look over her shoulder. Yep, Nick was angry. He was frustrated too, and there was something else on his face. It took her a moment to recognize it as determination, and that was new for him—well, not new, but she'd bet it was pretty damn rare.

Chapter Five

Men were slime, Emmy thought. And for once she wasn't thinking about Roger. Or Nick.

She was sitting in a crowded restaurant in the Leather District, a conglomeration of old leather factories that had been turned into businesses, lofts, restaurants and any other trendy, touristy use that could be found for them. Emmy would have preferred neighboring Chinatown, less fashionable but more relaxing. But here she sat at her best friend's insistence, nursing a cranberry martini, avoiding eye contact, waiting for Lindy to arrive. The prevailing demographic of the place seemed to be men, ranging in age from barely legal to one-foot-in-the-grave. She'd always considered men another species anyway; tonight she'd classify them as *homo erectus* rather than *homo sapiens*. That brought a smile to her face, and she had to drop her eyes to her drink before any of the Neanderthals took it as encouragement.

What was it with men anyway? When you wanted one to stick around, he left, and when you wanted one gone, you couldn't get rid of him. She looked around. And when you swore off men in general, they all seemed hell-bent to change your mind. Hopefully Lindy would show up soon. Or she could just leave, and the more she thought about it, the more appealing that sounded. She signaled the waiter, dug her cell phone out of her purse and speed-dialed Lindy, keeping a wary eye on the mood of the crowd in case any of these guys suspected she was about to bolt and worked up the courage to do more than ogle.

"I'm not really up for dinner tonight," she said when Lindy picked up.

"Uh-oh, what's wrong?"

"Nothing. I'm not hungry, and the only reason we were having dinner anyway is so I'd have an excuse for Nick."

"And here I thought it was my sparkling wit and sunny personality."

"You know what I mean, Lindy." They'd been out every night that week just in case Nick fell off the wagon and showed up at her house. "I appreciate you putting up with me all week, but I'm sure you have things to do. Or should I say men?"

Lindy snorted softly. "The only briefs in my life lately have been the legal kind, but you have been kind of cranky the last few days. Tonight you just sound depressed. Wouldn't be because of Nick, would it?"

"Nick isn't bothering me anymore."

"Yes, he is. Maybe not in the way you expected, but he's bothering you."

Emmy sighed.

"See? Case closed."

"Okay, so he's bothering me. He's not going to be the only one in a minute." Emmy had accidentally made eye contact with one of the cavemen and there was a definite shift in the mood of the crowd. If she didn't do something drastic…

Lindy walked in, took one look at Emmy's face and said, "if you kill me, who will represent you at the murder trial?"

"Actually I was thinking about giving you a big, wet kiss."

Lindy did a double take, then looked around, rolling her eyes as she took her seat. "If you're trying to put these hounds off with a little girl-on-girl action, think again," she said, shutting off her phone and dropping it into her purse. "You and your tongue come anywhere near me and we won't be able to beat them off with a stick. And what am I saying? I've been trying to attract a little male attention."

Emmy disconnected and put her phone away, too. "Is that why you picked this meat market?"

"Of course. You may have taken yourself out of the game, but I haven't. And speaking of games, what's the deal with Nick?"

"I don't want to talk about him." Emmy opened the menu and pretended she had an appetite. "You're just going to argue with me."

"Fine, let's talk about Roger. We agree about him."

Emmy looked up, caught Lindy smirking. "He called today. How did you know?"

"It was only a matter of time, Emmy. He wanted you back didn't he?"

"I don't know. I didn't return his call."

"Good, don't. And since we're through with Roger, we can get back to Nick."

Emmy sighed again before she could catch herself. "I'm just tired," she said before Lindy could put the look on her face into words. "It's been a long week."

"You're not tired, you're lonely. I'm not the solution to that problem, Em, but I'm here so you're stuck with me… Hello."

Emmy shifted in her seat so she could take in Lindy's field of vision. The busboy was heading for them, or rather for the circular booth next to their table. He bent to retrieve dishes and clean the tabletop, giving Lindy an up-close-and-personal shot of his really excellent backside. And she was enjoying it.

"He's about twelve," Emmy whispered behind her menu.

"He's at least twenty."

"And you're not really interested in him."

Lindy shrugged. "I can look can't I? It's never good to take life too seriously. I learned that the hard way—and you're changing the subject."

"You changed it first."

Lindy waved that off, which was just like her—now. She'd been nose-to-the-grindstone in college, all work and no play, until she'd broken under the weight of her own expectations. She'd had to go away for a while, to learn how to depressurize her life. Now she worked when it was time to work, and had fun everywhere else.

To those who didn't know Lindy, she'd seem like one of the most well-adjusted people in the world. The breakdown had left permanent damage, though. Lindy figured if she was such a perfectionist that she got that messed up over her career she'd better not risk love, let alone marriage and family. So, she'd become a serial dater, never hanging on to a relationship long enough to let it get serious. Emmy was one of the few who saw through her act, to the sadness and loneliness beneath.

"We were talking about Nick," Lindy reminded her.

"We were talking about me," Emmy said, because Lindy wouldn't thank her for turning the tables.

"It's the same thing, since he's the problem you're having."

"He's not a problem. He hasn't tried to kiss me again, and today he snapped at me."

"Oh, this is good." Lindy sat back in her chair and grinned—which was hardly the reaction Emmy had been going for, but the waiter arrived, and she decided to let it go.

"I'll have the chicken pasta."

"I'll have a double martini," Lindy said.

"You're not eating?"

"There are olives in the martini."

Emmy rolled her eyes.

"All right, I'll eat." Lindy smiled dazzlingly up at the waiter. "You choose for me," she said to him. "I'm sure whatever you give me will be incredible."

He froze for a few seconds, his eyes on Lindy, but Emmy had to give him credit for hanging on to his professionalism because he finally nodded and said, "Of course, ma'am." His words were a bit strangled, he wasn't breathing quite right, and his upper lip was sweating, but at least he didn't trip over his own feet the way she'd seen some men do after Lindy unleashed herself on them.

Emmy shook her head, but she was smiling, and it felt good. Trust Lindy to pull her out of the doldrums. "That man is never going to be the same."

"But my meal will be fabulous. Now, where were we? Oh, right, I was enjoying your upheaval."

"And I was about to call you a b—"

"Don't say it, you'll only feel terrible later."

"Not this time."

Lindy laughed off Emmy's scowl. "You have no reason to complain," she said. "Roger was considerate enough to go away before getting rid of him involved, well, hiring me. And five minutes later a drop-dead-gorgeous man walked into your life, stumbling all over himself the minute he laid eyes on you. If that wasn't lo—"

"Don't say it."

"Fine," Lindy huffed out, "but I'm using the other L-word because at the very least it was lust at first sight, and that's a pretty good place to start. If you had any sense you'd drag Nick Porter home, lock yourself in the bedroom with him for the next couple of weeks and see where it goes from there. My money's on happily ever after."

"No such thing," Emmy said.

"Then why were you marrying Roger?"

Emmy thought about that a minute, then did a hands-up. "The reason escapes me now."

"It doesn't escape me." Lindy took her martini out of the waiter's hand, barely sparing him a glance this time in favor of taking a big, fortifying swallow. "You don't want to be alone, but you don't want to take any emotional risks. You didn't love Roger, so he wasn't a threat. If you came home one day and found him gone, you wouldn't care."

"I'd care if he took all my furniture."

"And doesn't it mean anything to you that you'd miss your end tables more than your fiancé?"

"They're really nice end tables."

"Give me one good reason why you can't get together with Nick," Lindy said, the soft, wistful tone of her voice more compelling than all the exasperation that had gone before it.

Emmy picked up her drink and took her time fishing out the cherry.

"Well?"

"I'm thinking," she said. But everything she came up with was either ridiculous or something she couldn't say out loud. There was nothing wrong with Nick, unless you counted his low ambition quotient, and that was only a flaw to an over-achiever like her. The only real problem she had with him was that he made her want things she hadn't wanted in a long, long time. If she said that to Lindy, they'd be right back to exasperation because Lindy was a stop-griping-and-deal-with-it kind of person. Emmy didn't want to deal with this. She'd been lugging around her emotional baggage for years, and it hadn't gotten in her way. She didn't see any reason to unpack it now.

"You can think all you want," Lindy said, "but you won't come up with anything."

"Roger is gone, and Nick isn't taking his place."

"That sounds really convincing, but what are you going to do about you?"

Emmy shrugged.

"No, you don't," Lindy said, not letting her duck the subject. "Being a foster kid—"

"That's the past."

"Not if you keep letting it affect the present."

"I'm not going there tonight," Emmy warned.

"You never go there and it's unhealthy. One of these days you're going to wake up in a rubber room, missing a few months of your life."

"Do I get to pick which ones I want to forget?"

"No, and trust me, I know how it feels. I ignored my garbage until I was forced to deal with it. If you're smart, you'll deal with yours before that happens."

"I'm handling it fine."

"First you agreed to marry Roger for... I don't know the reasons, but I can tell you they were the wrong ones." Lindy leaned forward, keeping her voice down, "and now you're turning your back on a nice guy like Nick. Doesn't sound like dealing to me. It sounds like sticking your head in the sand."

"Whatever. It's working."

"For the time being," Lindy, the voice of doom, said.

Emmy looked away. She could tune Lindy out so she didn't hear the disapproval, and if she didn't look at her, she didn't have to see it, either. But she couldn't escape her own feelings—and suddenly she was feeling a whole lot. "You asked me to give you one reason why I shouldn't get together with Nick," she said. "How about he's scum?"

"No, he's not. You're just saying that because—"

"He's standing over there with a redhead," Emmy said, disgusted with herself more than Nick because she hated that he was standing there with any woman but her. "I told you he didn't want me anymore."

Chapter Six

Lindy twisted around in her chair, and saw what Emmy saw, Nick, standing in the vestibule, chatting with a beautiful, voluptuous redhead wearing barely enough clothing to keep her assets covered.

"Damn," Lindy said, "it would take three of my bras to corral those things."

Emmy wasn't much interested in the redhead. "*Scum* is probably not the word you'd choose," she said to her best friend, "but—"

"I don't know, Em." Lindy swung back around, not looking nearly convinced enough of Nick's scumhood to suit Emmy. "I think he's just talking to her, being friendly."

"Yeah, he's a friendly guy," Emmy muttered. "Not too choosy, but hey, nobody's perfect."

"Trying to find something wrong with him, are we?"

Emmy set her jaw and kept her eyes firmly averted.

"Whatever's going on with you, Emmy, you need to get a grip because he's headed this way. Alone."

Emmy couldn't help herself. She looked up and there was Nick, making a beeline for their table. He caught sight of her and smiled full-out. She'd braced herself, but it didn't do her much good. First her face flushed, then the warmth sank all the way to her curling toes, leaving behind some very notable hot spots. She picked up her water and took a long drink, the icy coolness of it sliding down into her stomach, which wasn't one of the body parts currently in need of temperature adjustment. Tearing her gaze off Nick helped a little; unfortunately her eyes landed on Lindy, who was smirking knowingly at her. Emmy refused to be embarrassed, which was easy considering she had other things to think about.

Like what the heck was Nick doing here anyway?

Either he read her mind or he saw the question on her face, because he said, "I couldn't help but notice where you were planning to have dinner tonight."

"That's what happens when you read over someone's shoulder," Emmy replied. "Stella was snooping in my day planner," she explained for Lindy's benefit, "and then Nick picked up where she left off."

"Looking for industrial espionage?"

"Just being nosy," Nick said, Lindy's sarcasm doing a fly-by, probably because he had yet to take his eyes off Emmy, and men weren't known for their ability to multi-task. It was a wonder the man could stare and talk at the same time, but somehow he managed it.

"You still haven't told us why you're here," Emmy said to Nick.

"The real question is, why am *I* still here?" Lindy was out of her seat before Emmy could do more than sputter out a reminder that she'd already ordered dinner. "Which I didn't really want in the first place," Lindy pointed out. "I'm sure Nick will love it—whatever it is." And she was gone.

Emmy watched her run the gamut of unattached wolves at the bar. When she turned back, Nick was in Lindy's chair. "Déjà vu," she said. "Except this time you weren't invited."

"You want Lindy to come back and protect you from me?"

No, Emmy thought, *I wanted Lindy to come back and protect me from myself.* Nick was sitting there, all handsome and smiling—a little scruffy, sure, but she was even beginning to like the two-day stubble. She wondered how it would feel if she ran her fingers through it, if it would be soft or scratchy against her cheek, and her lips—

"Tongue-tied?" he asked. "Anything I can do to help?"

Great, more mental pictures she had no business viewing. "We're not going to talk about me," she said, and she definitely wasn't thinking about her body parts anymore, especially not in any context that involved Nick.

"Okay," he said as the waiter arrived, "let's talk about me."

"Exactly what I had in mind." Emmy sat back a little so her meal could be set in front of her. The waiter hesitated, clearly disappointed, then he placed Lindy's plate in front of Nick. It was some sort of fusion cuisine in keeping with the trendy restaurant, a bristling tower comprised of asparagus, something white and mashed that may or may not have been potatoes, and what appeared to be thinly sliced beef. The whole thing was drizzled with some sort of brown sauce, and swirls of the same sauce decorated the white plate.

Nick turned it in a full circle, studying the tower from all sides, then picked up his fork and knocked it over.

No finesse, Emmy thought, but it wasn't his eating habits that offended her. "Don't have a lot of patience, do you?"

"Not when it's something I really want."

"Then I guess that means you don't really want to save your father's company."

Nick put down his fork, slowly, his face for once blank. Emmy had a suspicion that she'd said something wrong, but she couldn't imagine what.

"You've got me all figured out," he said, his smile teasing.

"Lindy help you with that, or were you studying more than my work flow this past week?"

"Lindy's a lawyer. She's learned to read people pretty well." Not to mention she'd had enough psychoanalysis to be able to sum up anyone in a couple of sentences. But Lindy's past was none of his business, and neither was Emmy's present. "I didn't need Lindy to tell me about you. You're obviously attached to your company, and the people who work there. You said yourself it's like a family."

"And that's bad?"

"Of course not," Emmy said, even if the concept of family was foreign to her—at least the concept of a happy family. "The problem is, you own the place, and that makes you responsible for everyone else who works there."

Nick abandoned his meal again, crossing his arms on the table and focusing intently on her. "I still don't see the problem."

"It's like being a parent. You can be a friend to your kids on occasion, but not all the time. Somebody has to provide stability and control, make the hard decisions even though it means the people affected by those decisions may be resentful or unhappy. That somebody is you, but you seem to be happy letting them run the show."

"Some of those 'kids' have been with Porter and Son since I was in grade school. They know the business better than I do."

"They know the back end—production and shipping. It's the front end of the business that's suffering, Nick. Sales, purchasing, product placement, advertising. That's your job, and you haven't been doing it very well. Hiring me is a good first step—"

"At least from eight to five."

Emmy sat back in her seat. She'd noticed his slight hesitation at signing the contract, and then promptly forgotten about it. There was no knowing what was going on in Nick

Porter's head, but she'd taken it for granted that he'd faced the fact that Porter and Son was in trouble. It appeared, however, that he wasn't entirely comfortable accepting help to rescue his company. She'd forgotten that some clients were like that, even after they'd hired her. She should have been more tactful, but she hadn't edited her opinions, and now he was on the defensive. "I'm sorry. I tend to get caught up in my work."

"That's your problem, isn't it?" Nick said. He didn't sound angry or vindictive, but he wasn't holding anything back, either. Not that she was in any position to criticize, considering she'd just done the same to him.

"You're all work, Emmy," he continued. "You don't know how to have fun."

"I can't afford to have fun. I own a business."

"So do I."

"For now."

Nick looked like he'd been slapped.

"I'm sorry, Nick, but it's not going to help you if I paint a nice, rosy picture."

"My banker has already done the gloom-and-doom speech. I can— I will get Porter and Son back in the black."

Bingo, Emmy thought. He didn't really want her help, he'd been coerced into hiring her. She pushed her plate away, considering something she'd never, ever considered before, something that made her feel like a failure. But maybe it was time to quit. Jobs didn't grow on trees, no doubt about that, but there was something about Nick…Sure, he was handsome, gorgeous actually, and she was attracted to him. But it wasn't the attraction that concerned her, the physical pull she felt whenever he was near—and sometimes when he wasn't. It was the way he tugged on her emotions she didn't like. Okay, it scared her, enough that her natural instinct for survival was kicking in, telling her to run before she tumbled into a state that would get her hurt.

Or perhaps it was too late for that. Letting Nick out of the contract meant consigning his company to bankruptcy, and if she could see how much Porter and Son meant to him, she could imagine how wrenching it would be for him to watch it die. And knowing he was hurting, knowing she might have done something to stop it, would hurt her.

Then there was her ego. She might be a total loss when it came to managing her personal life, but her profession was her life. It just wasn't in her to walk away, even from this big a challenge. The fact that Nick didn't welcome her interference only made her more determined to prove him wrong. And maybe she had something to prove to herself, too—that Nick wasn't really a problem, that she could resist him until the contract was completed and she never had to see him again.

Except Nick didn't feel like a problem, and never seeing him again didn't feel like a solution.

"Where did you go?" Nick asked quietly, the feel of his hand closing around hers more startling than any words he might have said. And more tempting.

It was all Emmy could do to formulate the will to pull away, let alone actually do it. But she did.

"Wherever you went, I guess you don't want company," Nick said. "Too bad. I'm great…company."

"You can't take anything seriously."

"Except you."

She preferred to take that as another joke. The fact that he was grinning unrepentantly helped. "If you want to save your father's company, you're going to have to start taking my advice seriously."

The grin disappeared. "I said I'd save it, and I will."

Emmy took some money out of her purse and laid it on the table, grateful he didn't argue or try to stop her when she stood. "Monday, Nick, we'll see if you can do more than talk."

"You only have three weeks left," he said. "That's what it says in the contract."

"Then we'd better not waste any time."

IT WAS raining Monday, a hard, soaking downpour that suited Nick's mood, which had been growing steadily gloomier since Friday night. The reason for his dismal mood could be summed up in one word. *Work.* It was the same word that had been plaguing him for most of his adult life, only this time it had an entirely different meaning. Before, work had meant Porter and Son, which stood in the way of his having a life of his own. Now it was in the way of him getting closer to Emmy.

She kept putting on the brakes, using work as an excuse, but he knew there was something else going on. He just didn't know what. But he intended to find out, and for once he was at his desk before Emmy came in. Waiting for her.

When his office door opened, though, it was Stella who came in. "Here's your coffee, Mr. Porter," she said, bustling over to set a steaming cup on his desk. "How about some breakfast? I've noticed you haven't been eating very well lately."

"No, thanks, just send Emmy in when she gets here."

Stella was halfway to the door when she turned back. "I know it's not my place, but…that efficiency expert is all wrong for you," she finished on a rush.

"You're right," Nick said, "it's not your place."

Stella drew herself up, resentful, wounded, just-trying-to-help-and-getting-no-appreciation-for-it. "I didn't think I'd ever see this day," she said, "but, just now, you reminded me of your father," and then she took herself back to her desk.

Nick didn't take her parting comment as a compliment. His father's demeanor had started at stern and worked its way down to churlish. He'd never raised his voice, but he could cut the legs out from under a person with nothing more than a look. There were some bright spots in Nick's memory—and his heart—playing catch, riding on his dad's shoulders, being tucked in at night. But those moments had been early in his life, while his mother was still alive and before he'd hit his teenage years and expectations had set in. The expectations had come along with some pretty harsh enforcement tactics: demanding good grades, screaming like a maniac at Nick's baseball games, taking the fun out of anything Nick enjoyed because nothing was more important than winning. And when Nick fell short, which was a lot of the time when the bar was set so high…Well, the good memories had become more like happy dreams than actual recollections.

He heard Emmy's voice in the outer office, and all he wanted was to take her in his arms, bury his face in her hair, and forget the past, even if it was the past that had brought her into his life. His father hadn't believed Nick could run the company and be nice to people at the same time. His father hadn't believed he could run it at all. Nick intended to prove him wrong, whatever it took.

Emmy appeared in his office doorway, soaking wet and sparkling from head to toe, and everything else became inconsequential.

"Somebody put glitter in my umbrella," she said, "and sabotaged it so it would open long enough to dump the glitter all over me and then become useless."

"I'll find out who did it," Nick said, simmering in the aftermath of thinking about his father, "and fire them."

"What good would that do?" Emmy asked, smiling in resigned amusement. "It'll only make them resent me more."

"At least let me apologize." Nick came around the desk, stuffing his hands in his pockets when he wanted to help her brush herself off. He was feeling kind of raw at the moment. If he touched her it wouldn't stop at the glitter, and for once he wasn't thinking in purely physical terms.

He'd never been one to dwell on his emotions, let alone share them. Come to think of it, he never had much emotional upheaval because he didn't take anything that seriously. Except his father, and for some reason talking to Emmy about it appealed to him. A lot.

Emmy didn't like the way Nick was looking at her. She tried to tuck her hair back behind her ears because he was staring at it, but she only managed to dislodge a shower of glitter. "I need to clean up before this stuff gets in my eyes," she said, escaping to the restroom off his office.

"You look pretty good to me," Nick said, following her. "Sparkly."

Emmy looked in the mirror, making a face at herself. Her hair was already drying, the untamable blond curls bouncing back to unruly—and shimmery—life. All she needed was grease paint, floppy shoes and a lapel flower that shot water and she'd be ready for the Big Top. Come to think of it, she could probably get all those items from Porter and Son's inventory. She could've asked Nick since he was currently standing about three feet behind her, his eyes glued to the mirror. "Stop looking at me like that," she said, trying not to wriggle and unable to stop herself.

"Can't help it," Nick said, "you're just so darn…cute."

Emmy whipped around. "I'm not cute."

Nick stepped forward, took her by the shoulders, and turned her to face the mirror again.

"Okay," Emmy said, grinning reluctantly at her own reflection, "I'm kind of cute, but this," she pointed to her face, "is misleading." She did a bit more wriggling and when that didn't do the job, she slipped off her jacket. "I'm a mess." She took her blouse by the collar and shook it, and when that only made the itch that much more unbearable, she untucked it and let a shower of glitter cascade to the floor.

"If you're going to take your clothes off, maybe I should lock the door first."

"I'm not taking anything off," Emmy said, absently brushing at her skirt.

Nick didn't answer, and when she glanced up she found him watching her dip her hand inside her clothing, over and over, to pull out the glitter that had sifted down into her waistband.

"You need any help with that?" he asked.

Yes was her first impulse. If he could make her that hot just by looking at her there was no telling what would happen if he put his hands on her. They'd probably both burst into flames.

She held his gaze, watched his eyes darken and drop to her mouth. He leaned in, and she didn't think she could live another minute without kissing him. But if she kissed him she wouldn't be able to stop. And she wouldn't be able to hide any longer. So she leaned back.

Nick closed the distance she'd put between them. He braced his hands on the sink on either side of her hips and for every inch she backed off, he advanced. They weren't touching, but she could feel his breath warm on her face, heating her lips. One of his legs slipped between hers, the rasp of the cloth across the bare skin on the inside of her knees almost unbearably sensual. Maybe a kiss would be all right, she thought, maybe it wouldn't ruin everything to indulge in one long, hot wet—

The sink tore out of the wall, it being an old building with old plumbing that wasn't up to Nick and Emmy's combined weight. They collapsed to the floor in a shower of water, stared at each other in shock for a few timeless seconds, then began to laugh uncontrollably.

Nick got up and pulled Emmy to her feet and right into his arms, but when he wanted to kiss her she turned her face away. Kissing him would be like setting off a bomb in her nice, tidy life, a flash of heat and brilliance that would destroy the orderly existence she'd created for herself, light the shadows and warm up the cold places, including the emptiness in her heart. Just the embrace brought tears to her eyes, and shook her to the foundations of who she believed she was. All it took was the feel of Nick's arms around her, the comfort and security of being held, for her to imagine that it would be all right to let go and trust him not to hurt her, to trust herself to work as hard as it took to make the relationship last forever. And to fear that it wouldn't be enough.

Losing Roger had been a blow to her ego. She had a feeling that losing Nick would be like a hit and run, indescribably brutal and something she'd never get over. But she had to let him into her life before she could lose him.

"I told you I was a mess," Emmy said, pulling away from Nick because it hurt too much to be in his arms when she knew she couldn't stay there.

She'd thought the water would hide her tears; she should have known he'd see the truth. What she hadn't been prepared for was the way his sympathy—no, she'd call it what it was—his pity, made her feel, and that was angry. "I'm no good with relationships. There I said it. There's something I don't do well. Roger was the longest I dated any man, and he dumped me less than a month before our wedding. Lindy is my only friend, and she's as bad at relationships as I am, so I figure we only tolerate each other because we don't want to be completely pathetic and alone."

"You don't believe that," Nick said. "You're friends because…well, I don't know why you're friends but it's not out of desperation. And you're not pushing me away because you're bad at relationships. Relationships just take work, which means you should be excellent at them. So what's holding you back?"

Emmy shut down, folded her arms and got that stubborn expression on her face. Nick liked that expression, the way she chewed on her lower lip, that little line between her eyes. He thought it was adorable. When they were working. "Are you really happy this way, Emmy? What's the worst that could happen if you take a chance on me?"

Emmy met his eyes, shook her head. "It's not you I'm taking a chance on."

Chapter Seven

Emmy went home to de-sparkle.

Nick stayed right where he was, shackled by his own belligerence to Porter and Son, Practical Jokes and Everyday Gags. The anger was back, bolstered by frustration, and propped up on a brand-new wave of determination not to let the company fail. He'd begun to think Emmy could help him, that he might have been a bit hasty in deciding to ignore her ideas before he'd even heard them. She wasn't doing anything drastic, mostly just common-sense things. His father wouldn't have had a problem with that, but while the old man would have applauded Emmy's common sense, he would have sneered at her profession. And hiring her in the first place would have spelled failure in his eyes.

Nick knew he could pull off a victory, but it was time to take off the kid gloves. Emmy was right about that, too, even if he'd had to come to that conclusion at his own pace. He walked into the factory and turned off the power at the main fuse box. Everything went dark and dead. The employees all milled around for a minute, wondering what had happened, before Nick was spotted and the place went deathly quiet. Very satisfying and dramatic, but there was still a point to drive home. "This is what it's going to be like around here if we don't do something," he said.

More silence, but the expressions on their faces and the looks they traded with each other said a lot, and Nick wasn't ignorant of the commentary. They'd never seen him like this before—he'd never been like this before. He could remember his father being angry lots of times, coldly furious, firing anyone who got in his way when he was on one of his rants. Nick might be determined to prove his old man wrong about his business acumen, but he'd be damned if he ran Porter and Son the way his father had, and that included the way he'd treated people.

The first order of business was admitting that a lot of his temper was actually frustration, and not just over the red ink. He'd been taking a hands-off approach to Emmy—for the most part—figuring she'd finish what she'd been hired to do, and work wouldn't get between them anymore. But his employees were holding things up, so the time had come for a little tough love. All around.

"Why don't you all go into the break room," he said, flipping the power back on and waiting until everyone had filed by him.

Nick followed them, stopping in the doorway because it was as good a place as any to address them from. "I'm sorry," he began. "I should have done this a long time ago, but… I guess I didn't say anything because I didn't want to worry anyone." And because he'd stuck his head in the sand, believing they were merely in a slump instead of a permanent turndown in business. "The company is in trouble. It has been for some time, and you deserve to know the truth. Either we turn things around or we won't last out the year. That's why Emmy's here."

"We can fix it ourselves," someone called out, echoed by comments like "Yeah, give us a chance," and "We don't need her."

"You got her," he said, raising his voice just loud enough

to be heard over the din. "And since she's trying to help us, we're going to stop getting in her way. Right?"

Wrong. There was some grumbling, a lot of sullen looks, but nobody was agreeing with the Stop-Hindering-Emmy plan.

"She's not leaving until she's ready to leave," Nick said. And not until she'd handed him a turnaround plan that would satisfy the loan officer down at the bank. "Live with it." He stomped back into the office, past Stella, ignoring her glare and the fact that she'd stayed in the factory to commiserate with the sulking horde.

Anger might not be the way to go, he concluded, but neither was nice. He'd been a friend as well as an employer all these years, and it hadn't gotten him anywhere. He didn't have to be as hard as his father, but he had some hard things to do and he decided he'd better do them before he lost his head of steam.

He picked up the phone and dialed information, staying on the line while he was connected with his number. Of all the drama he'd been through in the last hour, it was Emmy's parting comment that had stayed with him. He wasn't the best at figuring out women. Mostly he treated relationships like everything else in life, something to float through with the least possible amount of upheaval. Emmy was different. He liked the upheaval she caused—most of it anyway. If he could just figure out what was holding her back, he could get more of her brand of upheaval.

It's not you I'm taking a chance on, she'd said. Since there were only two of them involved, and he wasn't the problem, then she must be. And if she wouldn't tell him why she was a problem, then he'd have to find out for himself. And there was only one place he knew to go for answers.

"Talk fast," the person on the receiving end of his phone call said by way of greeting, "the clock is running."

Nick didn't remember the voice very well, since he'd been focused almost exclusively on Emmy the two times Lindy had been around, but he remembered the sarcasm. "Lindy? It's Nick. Nick Porter."

"I won't talk about Emmy behind her back," she informed him before there could even be any pleasantries.

"Maybe that's not why I called," Nick said, annoyed. "Maybe I need a lawyer."

"No, that's not it. You want to talk about Emmy."

"Are you always right?"

"Pretty much."

"I'll bet you're loyal, too, a good friend, someone who only wants the best for Emmy, even if it means crossing a line—"

"I see where you're going with this," Lindy said.

"And?"

She sighed. "Good thing you don't have the drive to be a lawyer."

"Who says I don't have drive? What is it with you women always wanting men to be ambitious? Once you're in a serious relationship with one of us, you complain we're not around because we're working too much."

"On second thought, I'm glad you don't *want* to be a lawyer."

"Does that mean I win?"

Silence, the kind made by an attorney looking for a loophole.

"You're thinking so hard I can smell the brimstone all the way over here," Nick said.

"Keep it up, wise guy, and you'll be talking to yourself." But Nick could hear the humor in her voice. "You win, but only because I have a client waiting in the lobby. And Emmy is my best friend. I want her to be happy."

"I want her to be happy, too."

"And you think you're the guy for the job?"

"I'd like to give it a try."

"Well, if you can't you're a hell of a candidate to force her to at least start working on her issues."

"Good," Nick said, relaxing marginally. Getting Lindy to talk to him was half the battle. Now he just had to convince her to help him. Behind her best friend's back. "Tell me everything."

"I don't know everything," Lindy said. "Emmy is pretty close-mouthed about her childhood. I know she was in foster care."

"She told me her parents died." And he'd been thinking she went to live with an aunt or grandparent, Nick realized. Instead, she'd been put into the care of strangers. From what little he knew of the foster system, it couldn't have been a picnic, even if Emmy hadn't been grieving. On the heels of such a traumatic loss, it wouldn't have taken much to make her close herself off completely. She thought she was sparing herself more pain, but she was only hurting herself worse. She just hadn't figured it out yet.

Nick had, and he couldn't bear the thought of her spending her life alone. Even if she ended up with Roger or some other bonehead, Nick wanted her to be happy, and until Emmy faced her past and found a way through it, she'd never be able to move on.

It lit a fire in him, for the first time in his life, knowing he might be able to help someone with a real problem, and he found himself all but dancing in place with the desperation to get started. All he had to do was convince Lindy to help him.

She'd been quiet, as caught up in her own thoughts as Nick had been. Now she said, "Emmy never talks about her real parents, let alone her foster ones."

"Can you put me in touch with them?" Nick asked. "The foster ones, I mean."

Lindy snorted out a slight, derisive laugh. "How do you want them, alphabetical or chronological order?"

Nick grimaced. "That many?"

"Quite a few—and that's all I know."

"No, it isn't."

"Yes, it is. Except I took enough psychology classes to know everything ties back to childhood."

Childhood and Mom, Nick thought. Or in his case, Dad.

"Foster records are sealed by the state," Lindy continued. "Even if I wanted to, I couldn't give you names. End of story."

"Wait," he said before she could hang up, "if you don't help me help Emmy, who will?"

"What makes you think Emmy's foster families are the key to helping her?"

"She's hiding from the past, Lindy—"

"She's protecting herself."

"She's locking herself away," Nick countered, "at least the part of her that really matters. Until she faces her memories, good and bad, she won't be able to get past them and move forward."

"And maybe she'll figure out it's time to take a chance on you?"

"Maybe she'll figure out it's time to take a chance on herself. To trust her heart again."

"Dammit," Lindy said, and Nick thought he heard her mutter something about throwing her own words back in her face.

"You know I'm right," he said.

There was another silence, this one humming with tension. "If you're asking what I think you're asking," Lindy finally said, "you're not just talking about the impossible, you're talking about jail time."

"Emmy's worth it."

"Easy to say when you won't be the one going to jail."

"I'll come visit you, bring you a cake with a file in it."

She chuckled, and Nick knew he had her.

"I guess the best I can hope for is that she won't press charges when she finds out," Lindy said, "and she *will* find out."

Lindy was right, and the thought of what Emmy was going to say should have made Nick think twice. But there was no way he'd let her give up on herself, even if it meant she'd never talk to him again.

"You're one of those make-lemonade-out-of-lemons people, aren't you?" Lindy asked into the silence.

"I'm more an ignore-the-lemons-and-they'll-go-away kind of guy."

"You're running the risk of Emmy going away," Lindy pointed out.

"I know." But it felt like more of a risk to stand back and not do anything.

WHEN Emmy got home she parked in front of her house. It wasn't where she usually parked, but she was in glitter hell. Everything itched, and the sooner she got inside, stripped and de-glittered herself, the better. Not that a shower was going to help her other problems, namely the havoc Nick had wreaked on her emotions.

It was bad enough that she'd had to face a few hard, sad truths about herself, she'd revealed some things to Nick she'd rather he didn't know. She preferred to keep her personal stuff to herself, but having her vulnerabilities exposed wasn't the problem. What Nick might choose to do with them was. He was determined to find a way around her defenses, and she'd just revealed a pretty big chink in her armor.

There wasn't a whole lot that could have made her day worse. Seeing Roger waiting on her front porch was one of them. With every inch of her body itching, she didn't have the time to talk to him. Or the patience.

"Hello, Emily," he said with an uncertainty that wasn't like the Roger she knew and…had no feelings about whatsoever, if she didn't count the mild level of annoyance.

"Hi," she said, unlocking her front door, stepping through, and shutting it in his face while he was too surprised to try to follow her inside. She heard a key working in the lock and yelled through the door, "I had it changed after you tried to steal my furniture."

"That was a cry for help," he shouted back.

"Funny, I thought it was robbery."

"I was trying to stay close to you, keeping things that were yours."

"Is that why you made a copy of the key?"

"It's my house, too," Roger said.

"Your name isn't on the deed." Thank God she hadn't added him yet—or more accurately, thank Lindy for not allowing her to add him until after the wedding.

"I paid half the mortgage for the last six months," Roger shouted, sounding like himself again, irritated and demanding.

"And what, you expect me to pay you back?"

"I don't want you to pay me back, but you have to admit I'm out some money. I imagine a court would see it that way."

"So now you're threatening me?"

There was silence for a beat or two, then, "You're right," he said, "I'm sorry."

Emmy exhaled heavily, letting some of her impatience go at the same time. Roger sounded as wrung-out as she felt. He looked it, too, when she peeked through the sheers covering the bow window in the front.

"I need to talk to you," he said almost too quietly for her to hear through the door.

She actually considered it for a second or two before she came to her senses. Sympathy was one thing; it would be stupidity to let Roger through the front door. "No."

Roger's shoulders slumped, and he raised a hand, resting just his fingertips on the door.

Sympathy crept back over her, accompanied by guilt. She was on the verge of relenting when he looked over at the window. Emmy jumped back; she didn't think he'd seen her, and she ought to talk to him because probably she was only putting off the inevitable. But she was just too tired to face him.

"Emily? Please let me come in."

"Not tonight. I had a rotten day."

"I've had a rotten week," he said. "I need to talk to you about the wedding plans."

"Fine, call me tomorrow and we'll set something up, okay?"

"Okay." He walked away, still looking as dejected as he'd sounded.

Emmy's hand was on the doorknob when her cell phone rang. She looked at the display, laughing softly at her own gullibility. "You must have radar," she said to Lindy by way of greeting. "Roger was just here, and I almost let him in."

"You didn't, right?"

"No, but he sounded pretty pathetic. I think I should call him and set up a lunch."

"That's exactly what he wants, Em, you feeling guilty so he can suck you back in."

"He needs to talk to me about the wedding plans, and I really did dump everything on him."

"He dumped you, you dumped on him. Sounds fair to me."

"What can it hurt, Lindy?"

"He wants you back. His new girlfriend probably kicked him to the curb already."

That stopped her. "How do you know that?"

"Okay, I don't know that, but what if I'm right? What are you going to do if he says he was an idiot? Besides agree with him."

"Roger would never admit…"

"He said he was wrong for dumping you, didn't he?"

"Not in those words."

"In what words?"

"He said trying to steal my furniture was a cry for help, that he was just trying to keep something of mine close."

"A normal man would settle for panties," Lindy muttered. "What else did he say?"

Emmy gave her a quick rundown of the interchange, and Lindy said something uncomplimentary about Roger's physical endowment—not far off the mark, actually—and it made Emmy smile, which was better than feeling like an idiot. "Maybe I should give him his money back," she said. "At least then he'd go away."

"You give in on this and he'll only want something else the next time. Come to my office on Saturday. You can sign a power of attorney giving me control over the house. I'll call Roger and throw my legal weight around a little, get him to back off."

"Okay, but how will a power of attorney get rid of Roger?"

"Are you a lawyer?"

"No."

"Then let me worry about the house. Once Roger is gone we'll tear it up."

There was something in Lindy's voice… She'd hurt Lindy's feelings, Emmy realized. "I'm sorry, Lindy, you know I trust you."

"Yeah," Lindy sighed. "I know you trust me. Look, you own the house. Roger has no legal claim over it because you were never married."

"But he did pay half the mortgage while he lived here, and he can take me to court—"

"And if he does that you can slap him with a nice, fat rent bill."

"Do you think that'll be enough to make him go away?"

"That's what the power of attorney is for. I'll get him to sign off on any claim to your house, and you won't ever have to see him again."

"I don't know. It feels kind of mean to sic my lawyer on him."

"It will also send a message."

Emmy blew out a breath. "You're right, Lindy. I owe you big-time for tackling Roger for me. And thanks for listening to me whine about Nick, and for all the times—"

"Emmy?"

"What?"

"I always have your best interests at heart. You know that, right?"

"Of course I do. I feel the same way about you. If there's ever anything you need—"

"You'll be there. I know. Kiss, kiss, hug, hug. We'll dispense with Roger on Saturday. Come for lunch and I'll buy you a big martini."

"Better make it a virgin…something or other," Emmy finished, because you couldn't get a virgin martini and she couldn't come up with anything nonalcoholic at the moment. "I'm going to a charity function with Nick and I can't deal with him after I've been drinking." Alcohol lowered inhibitions and hers already weighed a ton when Nick was around. Any handicap at all and she wouldn't be able to hold them up for long.

"Charity function?" Lindy asked, "When did you agree to that?"

"It's in the contract, actually. Part of my job is to help him refine his process, and to do that I need to know which products are popular and which aren't. Nick donates excess inventory to this charity every year and I thought it would be a good place to do some informal polling of his target audience."

"It's not the Annual Children's Fair in the Park?"

"That sounds right."

"Get the martini," Lindy said. "Get two. I have a feeling you're going to need them."

Chapter Eight

Saturday, Emmy met Lindy at a place that Roger hated, and none of Nick's employees were likely to frequent. It was the first time she'd relaxed completely in two weeks.

They dispensed with the power of attorney straight away, then settled in to have a meal that didn't include any talk of work or men—until Nick invaded their man-free space by calling Emmy's cell phone.

"What are you doing?" he asked.

"Pest control," Emmy said.

"Termites?"

"A rat. A really big one."

"You can stay with me," he offered.

"Not necessary," she said, "the rat is gone, and Lindy is going to make sure he doesn't come back."

"He? I'm missing something, aren't I?"

"Yes, but it's nothing important." She consulted her day planner, even though she knew her memory wasn't faulty. "We aren't meeting until two."

"I couldn't wait. Where are you?"

"In South Boston, having lunch with Lindy," she said and gave him the name of the old, family-owned Irish pub where they were. The tourist crowds were smaller there, if not nonexistent, and no one cared if they lingered over their meal for a couple of hours.

"Hmm… What are you two talking about?"

"Not you, if that's what you want to know. Men are off limits." Well, except Roger, but that didn't count because that was a conversation about how to make him go away, permanently. "We're pretty much done not talking about men, so I can head over there—"

"Nope," Nick said. "The fair is in East Boston, so you're right on the way."

Which was another of the reasons Emmy had chosen this pub.

"It's better if we drive together," Nick was saying. "Parking is limited at the fair, and this way we won't have to worry about where we're meeting up."

"Fine, I'll drive with you," Emmy agreed, because he obviously wasn't taking no for an answer. "No monkey business."

"How about monkey sex?" Lindy suggested.

"Cut it out," Emmy said, covering the phone so Nick wouldn't hear her and want to know what she was talking about. She could have made something up, but the truth was the idea of monkey sex—or any sex—with Nick had all but destroyed her ability to think, and what brain cells were still operating had gotten all wound up in imagining Nick doing things to her she'd only heard about on *Sex and the City*.

"Only in that it pertains to work," Nick said.

"What?"

"You could say my business is monkey business."

Emmy dragged her mind up out of the gutter, and since Lindy was rolling her eyes and making faces, she closed up her day planner, and carted it outside to finish the conversation. "Sounds like a loophole to me," she said to Nick on the way to the sidewalk.

"You've been spending too much time with Lindy. You need some variety in your life."

"I know what Lindy wants. You're a mystery."

"Not really. You know what I want, too."

"And this is supposed to convince me to spend the afternoon with you?" But Emmy was flattered and amused, and there was a pain in her chest for some inexplicable reason. It almost made her change her mind about going with him. Being wanted shouldn't hurt.

"I promise to keep my hands to myself," Nick said.

"Just your hands?"

"All my body parts."

Nick pulled up to the curb and bounded out of the car, positively beaming at her. "Turns out I wasn't far away when I called," he said. "You look great."

Emmy shut off her phone and looked down at her sleeveless tank, jean skirt and strappy sandals. The clothing was right for an outdoor fair, but she wasn't sure about her footwear. "Do you think I need different shoes?"

Nick gave her a nice, long onceover, and any reluctance she had about going with him evaporated. She really shouldn't like the way he looked at her so much. She knew it was dangerous, but she couldn't help feeling…beautiful. And sexy.

"You're perfect," Nick said.

"You know, eyes are a body part, too."

He put his hands up. "Just looking, not touching."

But it felt like it, Emmy thought.

"Well, look who's here," Lindy said, coming out of the restaurant. "Aren't you just rarin' to go?"

Nick never took his eyes off Emmy. "All it takes is the right motivation."

"That's what they say in the D.A.'s office. Let's hope it doesn't come back around to bite you in the ass."

Emmy reared back, staring at Lindy. "What's that supposed to mean?"

"Nothing," Lindy said. "C'mon, Emmy, we should be going."

Emmy stayed put, still staring, still puzzled. Lindy had been pushing her at Nick since the day they'd met, and now, suddenly, she was trying to drag her away?

"Emmy is coming with me," Nick said, taking her by the elbow.

"Hey, you were going to keep your hands to yourself," Emmy reminded him.

Lindy started to say something, Nick turned on her, the expression on his face saying Back Off.

"Fine," Lindy said to Emmy, "go with him, it'll be good for you."

"Don't I have any say in this?"

Nick hustled her into his car almost before she finished the sentence, racing around to hop in the driver's side and get in motion as quickly as possible.

"This was my idea in the first place," she reminded him, "I'm not going to back out." But that was before she found out where he was taking her.

They wound their way out of the still predominantly Irish neighborhoods of South Boston, across the harbor to the peninsula that made up one of the oldest neighborhoods in the city. East Boston had begun as five islands that were eventually connected with landfill, and now boasted Logan Airport and Suffolk Downs. It had always been an area populated by immigrants; these days families from Italy, South America and Asia settled in the community.

Nick navigated to one of East Boston's large open areas, which wasn't quite so open anymore. Emmy spotted the amusement park rides, the Ferris wheel and roller coaster, long before she got close enough to see the banner announcing it as the Annual Children's Fair in the Park. And way before she managed to read the fine print under the big words.

She'd known they were going to a children's charity fair, but while children had always made her sort of generally nervous—they were so unpredictable—this particular classification of children actually made her nauseous. Nick parked the car, came around and opened her door, but she didn't get out. She just sat there in the passenger seat, watching the kids run around and trying not to lose her lunch. Or cry, which would be so much worse.

"Emmy?"

"I thought this was a charity for sick kids."

"Underprivileged," Nick said. "Is that a problem?"

Hell, yes, it was a problem. The place was crawling with foster kids, foster parents and social workers.

Nick squatted down so he was at eye level with her. "Tell me what's wrong."

The only thing worse than walking into a maze of bad memories would be telling Nick about her childhood and seeing the concern on his face turn to pity. Emmy plastered on a smile and said, "You're in my way."

"Seriously, Emmy, if you don't want to be here—"

"Don't be silly. They're only kids, and it's wonderful that you're helping them."

"Then what's wrong?"

"Tomorrow when they wake up their problems will still be the same."

"But at least for today they can forget about their troubles."

That was Nick, a live-in-the-moment kind of guy.

"You sound like you have some experience with these kids," he said.

"I do, and they need all the help they can get, so let's go spend some money."

IT WAS a typical fair, with the typical rides and the typical booths selling cotton candy or chances to win a goldfish or a stuffed animal of monstrous proportions. Some of the game booths, all the rides and limited refreshments were free for the children. Adults were charged, with the proceeds going to the charity. Once Emmy got past the initial shock she actually sort of enjoyed herself.

If there'd been anything like this when she was a kid it would have been a nice escape. Nick was right about that. True, her life wouldn't have improved noticeably because of the fair, but at least for a few hours she'd have been able to leave behind the day-to-day loneliness, the constant need to guard against letting herself get too comfortable where she was, the certainty that she was on her own, even when she was surrounded by people.

For a little while she'd believed Roger would save her—from being alone, at least. But he'd turned out to be like everyone else who'd left her behind. Or maybe she'd gotten so good at guarding her heart she didn't know how to let people in anymore, and sooner or later they had no choice but to walk away.

"Recognize any of the prizes?" Nick asked her.

Emmy looked up at him and felt the heart she'd thought was locked so tight begin to creak open, painfully, before she slammed it shut again. She could fall in love with him so easily, if she wasn't careful, and not because of the hand-some, sexy package. It was the man inside the package, the Nick who wouldn't let her shut him out, no matter how many times she tried.

She wasn't ready to let him in just yet, but she was afraid, very much afraid, she was headed there, and to hell with the risk.

"Emmy?"

She smiled, focusing her attention on the here and now, on the whoopee cushions, bouncy balls and plastic bowling sets hanging from the overhead hooks of a nearby booth, a booth that was crowded with children under the age of ten. None of them left empty-handed.

"Looks like the pirate hats and plastic samurai swords are pretty popular," she said. "It was a great idea to come here and see how the kids react, and not just to your products. You can see how items from other manufacturers are going over, maybe consider some changes to your product line."

Nick's smile faded. "Changes?"

"The plastic bowling sets and bouncy balls aren't going, for instance."

"We've been making those for forty-five years, since…"

"Since your father started the company?" Emmy didn't have that kind of legacy to give her life foundation, but that didn't mean she couldn't understand how important it was to Nick. It was her job, though, to make sure nothing got in the way of saving Porter and Son, and that included sentiment. "Times change, Nick, you have to change with them or you'll be left behind."

"My father could've made it work."

Aha, she thought, *so it isn't nostalgia driving him to save Porter and Son, at least not entirely.* Pride was involved, too. She would've said pride was the last thing Nick would let motivate him. He was the least egotistical man she'd ever met. Yet she could see he was ready to dig his heels in at the notion of changing his product line, and she wasn't in the mood to take him on. She'd meant what she'd said about it being necessary to save the company. But it wasn't necessary today.

"We can talk about it Monday," she said, "the important thing is that the kids are having a wonderful day, and you helped make it possible. Isn't that why you're really here?"

"Partly."

He took her hand, pulled her over to one of the games and let her go before she could feel anything more than disappointment that the skin-to-skin rush didn't last nearly long enough.

Nick slapped a twenty on the counter and made a bring-it-on gesture. The carnie dropped a basket of balls in front of Nick and stepped back. Nick took aim and let fly with one ball after another. The trio of weighted milk bottles crashed to the floor each time. He took the huge purple gorilla the carnie handed him and promptly passed it along to the first child walking by, a little boy about four years old.

The boy looked at the woman holding his hand, waited until she nodded before he accepted the gorilla, huge brown eyes rounding.

"Thank you, Mr...."

"Porter," Nick supplied, taking the hand the woman held out.

"Mr. Porter," she said, dropping her voice and looking down to make sure the boy was too engrossed in his newfound stuffed friend to hear her. "Charlie has had a pretty rough time. My husband and I are planning to adopt him, but he's so...guarded. Unexpected generosity like yours, the kind that doesn't ask for anything in return, is so important in helping him understand that everyone isn't bad."

Nick hunkered down in front of Charlie, who dragged his attention off the gorilla and stared warily back at Nick.

"This guy needs a home, too," Nick said, tweaking the gorilla on its bulbous black nose. "I'm counting on you and this nice lady to give him one."

Charlie hugged the gorilla closer, nodding solemnly.

"Say thank you, Charlie," the woman instructed.

"Thank you," he echoed dutifully.

The real gratitude was in his eyes, and it brought tears to Emmy's.

"C'mon," Nick said, holding out his hand, "let's go see how many of those purple things we can give away today."

"I like the green ones, too," Emmy said, "and the pink ones, and the orange ones." She fell into step with him, but she didn't take his hand. Just being around him was dangerous enough.

They played more games, gave away more stuffed animals and goldfish, and they were being followed by a regular parade of hopeful children.

"I hope you brought a lot of money," Emmy said, smiling at the first rank of kids.

"Actually, I'm about tapped out," Nick said, showing her his empty wallet. He turned out both pockets and came up with a handful of coins, which he took over to a bank of nearby claw machines.

The crowd of kids pressed close, noses to the glass, watching Nick try and miss the first time. A ragged chorus of disappointed "awwws" muffled the sound of him poking the last of his money into the machine.

"Now or never," he said to Emmy. He finessed the joystick to put the claw right where he wanted it, leaned back a little to judge its placement, and let it drop. The claw folded inward and lifted, a necklace of plastic beads hanging from one talon and a clear plastic ball nestled in the center. It jerked and shuddered its way back, the kids oohing and aahing until the claw made it safely home, dropping the loot down the chute instead of back into the machine.

Nick reached in and immediately the children began to clamor. "Nope," he said over the din, holding up both hands to gain a measure of quiet. "This is for my lady friend." But instead of putting the beads around Emmy's neck, he doubled up the strand and laid them on top of her curls. "There's nothing like a crown to make a girl feel like a princess," he said winking at the crowd of kids, making girls blush and boys dig their feet into the dirt in embarrassment. He opened the plastic ball and a flimsy gold-colored ring fell into his open palm. And his face lit with that devilish smile. "And you can never go wrong with jewelry."

He turned toward her with that ring, and Emmy fisted both hands. No way was she letting him put a ring on her, even a cheap carnival one.

"You have to take it," Nick whispered. "You'll disappoint the kids. Especially the girls."

"Give it to one of them."

"You're not going to reject me in front of all these people?"

Emmy took in the crowd, the dreaminess in the eyes of the little girls, not to mention the foster mothers standing behind, more than one of whom looked a little misty. She didn't believe in fairy tales, especially for kids who too often learned there was no such thing, but she couldn't bring herself to be the one to disappoint them.

She unfisted her hand—her right hand—and let Nick slip the ring over her pinkie, which was the only place it fitted. The kids clapped and cheered, and looked longingly toward the booths, the moment of mushiness already forgotten.

"Now I'm broke," Nick said, "and there's going to be a riot in about two minutes."

Emmy opened her purse, the plastic necklace falling off her head and into it when she looked inside. She pulled out every last dime she had on her, but when she tried to hand it to Nick, he wouldn't take it.

"Uh-uh," he said, "it's your money, you have to play."

"I'm terrible at these things," Emmy said, "and you haven't lost once."

Nick shrugged. "I spent a lot of time at these fairs when I was a kid. It was kind of the family business, after all."

"Really, Nick," Emmy whispered, glancing over her shoulder, "I don't want to let them down."

"You won't," Nick assured her.

"If you say so." Emmy sighed and followed him to the next booth, doing a preemptive hands-up for the benefit of the crowd.

The game consisted of bushel baskets, turned on their sides and tipped up just slightly. The goal was to toss a softball into the basket without it bouncing back out again. Three balls in won. It looked simple. It took Emmy exactly one toss to realize looks were deceiving.

"Here, let me show you." Nick moved in close behind her, cupped her palm, which was holding the ball, and guided her toss so that the ball skimmed the top of the basket and dropped straight into the bottom. It bounced, but it bounced straight up before settling in.

Two more tosses, two more balls settling into the basket. The booth operator declared her the winner, but Emmy didn't hear because Nick was pressed against her from knees to shoulder blades, and her head was spinning so fast she lost her balance just standing in place. Nick wrapped an arm around her waist to steady her, and she could tell he was every bit as worked up as she was.

She jerked away from him and moved off, her hands pressed to her burning cheeks. Nick stepped up to the counter, chose a stuffed animal, and handed it off to one of the waiting children. Emmy didn't miss the fact that he stayed put for a good ten minutes, and he suddenly had no problem spending the rest of her money, as long as doing it gave him full frontal concealment. By the time her money was gone they'd both gotten control, and the fair was beginning to wind down.

None too soon, Emmy thought, moving off beside him again, this time heading for his car. "Maybe you could come up with countertop versions of some of these games," she suggested, "something inexpensive that captures the innocent fun."

"It's been done already," Nick said.

"There has to be a way to put a new twist on it. Have you ever explored the possibilities of adding gaming to your catalog?"

"Kids these days want video games," he said, sounding slightly annoyed.

"Really?" Emmy looked around. "There aren't any video games around, and these kids seem to be having a lot of fun."

Nick glanced over at her. "You might want to give it a try yourself."

"What's that supposed to mean?"

"Can't you talk about anything but business?"

"That's why we're here," she pointed out.

Nick didn't have a comeback for that, and how could he when she was right? And nervous and afraid.

Nick was keeping his distance, but she could feel his eyes on her when he didn't think she was paying attention. She'd experienced this rush of heat from the first moment he'd looked at her, but now she knew how it felt to actually be touched by him. The warmth of his skin, the strength of his arms around her, to have his lips no more than a breath away, so close, heart and body ached with the need to bridge that tiny gap, even while fear held her back.

Fear wasn't talking quite so loudly anymore, though, or perhaps her desire was shouting louder. Emmy wanted Nick's hands on her. The need swimming in her blood was nearly unbearable. The craving wound tighter and tighter inside her, and reason was slowly losing the battle to impulse because some time in the last few hours her thoughts had shifted from preventive to justifying. Her brain kept finding loopholes in her personal involvement moratorium, and it was getting easier and easier to give herself permission to step through those holes.

"I should get home," she heard herself say, a last-ditch effort to focus on something, anything but Nick's car, of spending twenty minutes alone with him only inches away. It wasn't a big car, but the seats reclined and she was pretty flexible from all the libido-adjusting yoga she'd been doing. Sex in those seats was entirely possible, even monkey sex—

"Emily?"

She almost didn't stop, even when Nick slowed and searched the crowd behind them. She didn't know anyone at the fair, and she only used Emily in her professional life. Who was she kidding? Monkey-sex fantasies aside she didn't have a personal life. Everyone except Nick and Lindy called her Emily.

Including her foster parents.

Chapter Nine

"Emily Jones!"

Emmy kept walking. No way was she turning around.

Nick put his hand on her arm, just long enough to short-circuit her system so she forgot why she was hell-bent on making it to the car. Her name floated above the din of the crowd again. She turned and saw an elderly woman making her way through the throng behind her, waving and calling her name.

Her brain still hadn't kicked in, so she searched the faces of the people around her, but everyone else was focused on their little groups. She looked at the old woman again, struggling to recognize the kindly face, the gray hair twisted up into a bun, *something* about this woman who looked like Mother Goose and rang no bells whatsoever in her Nick-fuddled brain.

"Emily?" the woman said again, waiting for a couple with two small children to pass between them before she stepped closer. "It *is* you. I thought so, but you were only twelve the last time I saw you."

Emily stared at her, mind racing, heart palpitating, palms sweating.

"It's Mrs. Runion, dear. You came to live with me when you were, oh, nine, ten years old. Of course, I didn't have gray hair then—well, I had a few but a few can be dealt with. Once it began to feel like a losing battle I decided to stop fighting nature."

Emmy had drawn in a breath when she heard the woman's name, and she had yet to let it out. Her throat seemed to have closed up, or maybe her heart had jumped up so high in her chest there wasn't room for air or words—or willpower, considering that when Nick steered her to the nearest table she sat down like an idiot.

Mrs. Runion took the chair across from her. Emmy looked around frantically, but Nick had moved off a little way, out of earshot. She could feel his eyes on her, though, and not in the way she'd come to appreciate. Why he should be worried about her having a conversation with an old woman was beyond her, but she didn't have time to figure it out right at that moment.

"How have you been, dear?" Mrs. Runion asked, overlooking the fact that Emmy was on the verge of asphyxia.

But then, Mrs. Runion came from the ignore-it-and-it-will-go-away school of foster parenting. She'd never been one to acknowledge the unpleasant. In fact, she'd always gone out of her way to avoid the mere possibility of trouble.

Mrs. Runion had been her foster parent from the time Emmy was ten until she was nearly twelve, at which time Emmy had been sent back to the state because Mrs. Runion didn't keep children past a certain age—and size. By the time Emmy was nearing her twelfth birthday she was already taller than Mrs. Runion. Not that Emmy blamed her. Some of the kids in the system were scary at any age, and when they got some size… Best to say she could understand a petite woman's concern.

Other than that, Mrs. Runion had run a clean, if cluttered, house. She'd been politely distant, and she always seemed to be vaguely confused by the lot of the children in her care, as if there must be something wrong with a child nobody wanted.

To a kid who'd secretly believed her parents wouldn't have died if she'd deserved them, it had been devastating. Mrs. Runion's hadn't been the worst foster home Emmy had been in, by far, but she'd been happy to leave there and never again have to see that perplexed look on the woman's face, to search inside herself trying to figure out what she'd done wrong to put it there.

"I'm fine," Emmy finally said. That pretty much exhausted the conversational possibilities, but Mrs. Runion was still staring at her.

"You look…all grown up," Mrs. Runion said, her eyes going to Emmy's unruly curls as though she was itching to pin them back, as she used to do. "You graduated from high school?"

"And college," Emmy said, wondering if Mrs. Runion was thinking that an orphan shouldn't be allowed to go to college.

"I'm glad to see you're doing so well."

"I have to go." Emmy stood, thrilled to find her legs would actually hold her.

"Oh, yes, well, I should be rounding up my charges as well," Mrs. Runion said. "It was nice to see you, dear."

Emmy set off for the car, taking one deep breath after another, despite the sharp pains in her chest. She'd survived her childhood and it would be foolish to let a chance encounter destroy a wonderful afternoon.

She wasn't about to cry in front of Nick, either. Not because tears would make him uncomfortable, because he was a natural caretaker. If he saw her crying he'd want to put his arms around her and if he put his arms around her there was no telling what she'd do, considering her fragile emotional state.

"Want to talk about it?" Nick asked her when she'd caught up with him.

"No." Absolutely not. It wasn't the possibility that she'd end up crying on his shoulder, what really worried her was whether or not she'd be naked when she did it. "She was just an old…teacher of mine."

She could tell Nick knew she wasn't being honest, and it hung there between them on the ride back to the downtown parking structure where she'd left her car. By the time they pulled into the empty slot beside her Focus, Nick was good and ticked off.

"Obviously something about that woman upset you," he said, "and you're not going to talk about it at all?"

"It's none of your bus—"

Nick slid a hand around the back of her neck, pulled her close and kissed her, a chaste kiss that was over before she could feel more than shock. "That makes it my business," he said, his face barely an inch from hers. "And that's something else you're going to have to deal with, whether you want to or not."

Emmy stared back at him a minute, then pounced, the physical desire that had been simmering inside her all day mixing with the emotional need that had flared up when she ran into her past. She wanted Nick's arms around her, to comfort and to help her forget.

He was only too willing to oblige. The kiss grew hot and heavy—as hot and heavy as it could in a car with bucket seats and a console the size of Cape Cod. Emmy wasn't letting that stop her.

Nick, however, did, by putting her back in her seat, getting out of the car and coming around to her side. When he opened the door she was waiting for him to pick up where they'd left off, but he just stood there.

"What's wrong?"

"Nothing. Everything."

"If you don't want me," Emmy began, stepping out of the car.

He moved back, scrubbing a hand over his face. "It's not that. When we do this we're going to do it right, and for the right reasons."

"It's just—"

"Don't. If you know what's good for you right now you won't say this is just sex or try to pretend there's not something between us that you can't tidy up with your schedules and lists and contracts."

Emmy stood there for a second, then tried to fish her keys out of her purse, mostly by touch since her vision seemed to be blurring for some reason. She finally found them, beeped the car open and got in, starting the engine immediately. She wasn't feeling quite steady enough to drive, but she knew Nick wouldn't leave until she did, and she needed to get away from him. He was right, her schedules and lists weren't going to save her from him. And nothing about the situation was going to be tidy.

SATURDAY NIGHT dragged by, eight interminable hours of sleeplessness while Emmy's thoughts spun in circles like a dog chasing its tail. Every once in awhile she'd fallen asleep for a few precious minutes, dropped like a stone into a deep, dark place that started out peaceful and then filled up with the most amazing dreams she'd ever had. Hot, steamy, X-rated dreams, and Nick was the star of the show. Starting with the way he kissed.

The only thing that would have made it better was if he'd actually been there with her. At least she'd have lost sleep for real orgasms instead of waking up in a sweat, breathless and needy and frustrated, just before the big payoff.

Hours before the alarm sounded Monday morning she was

awake yet again, nerves throbbing, all wound up and nowhere to go with it. Two nights and one day had passed since
the charity fair, approximately forty hours, give or take. She'd
slept maybe three of those hours, altogether. She could try to
go back to sleep, but tossing and turning for the next couple
of hours didn't hold any attraction.

Yoga might help burn off the desire, or aerobics or a brisk
three-mile run, but this wasn't just desire. It was lust. Pure,
unadulterated, industrial-strength lust. Way beyond the ability
of mere exercise to cure. If this kept up, the only way to get
Nick off her mind would be a lobotomy.

Or she could make a list. A list seemed like just the thing
to get her back to some frame of mind and condition of body
that felt…normal. It sounded simple. It was anything but.

There wasn't a whole lot wrong with Nick, but the list
wasn't really about him. It was about her. She was afraid of
love. That was the most difficult thing she'd ever had to write
down, but once she managed that single short sentence, the
reasons poured out of her.

She didn't really remember her parents. They'd died when
she was too young to have anything left of them but impres-
sions, feelings of safety and comfort. And love, she guessed.
At least that had been the one thing she'd wanted the most
every time she was placed in a new foster home. For years
she'd managed to hold out the hope that somebody would
love her. Eventually she'd given up—and then she'd gone in
the other direction, shying away from love. Roger had been
tolerable because she hadn't loved him, but Nick was another
story. She couldn't get involved with Nick because if he left,
she'd be devastated.

That was the end of the list. But not the dreams. Or the
sleepless thought-circling thing. She wasn't up to facing Nick,
so she stayed away from Porter and Son on Monday, hoping

another twenty-four hours would do the trick. It didn't, but she had a job to do. And she could be professional—she added it to her list just in case—and if Nick even looked her way she'd concentrate on work and pretend she'd never fantasized about him like…that.

She did her normal morning exercise routine—a bit of light resistance work since it was Tuesday. She ate her normal breakfast—oatmeal, whole grain toast, orange juice—and then she put on her shortest skirt, let her hair go curly and wild, and considered glitter. Briefly. If glitter was what turned Nick on, she wisely decided, he should go back to junior high. Come to think of it, the skirt had to go, and her hair was way too out of control. She did the best she could there; unfortunately she still had at least an hour to kill, so she stopped for coffee at the same coffee shop she stopped at every morning. But for once she took her time drinking it.

Sitting outside in the bright summer morning, sipping her coffee, watching the world rush by, was a new experience for Emmy. Usually she was the one racing from point A to point B at top speed, not paying the least bit of attention to what she passed on the journey. The destination was everything, and the faster she got there the better.

For the first time she realized she wasn't running to something, she was running away from everything, from her own childhood. From who she was.

"Is this seat taken?"

Emmy looked over. She'd been sitting sideways at a little table with a grated metal top. A man had his hand on the chair that would have been to her left, but was, instead, behind her. The hand looked like it belonged to a laborer, rough, the nails stained and bitten down to the quick. His clothes were worn, but no more worn than any teenager shuffling around with his jeans at half-mast and his pant legs dragging the ground. He had dark hair and unremarkable features, and his expression was pleasant and slightly questioning as he waited for her answer.

Politeness had Emmy nodding to him to sit, but there was something about him, something hard and considering, that made her sit up a bit straighter, slug back the rest of her lukewarm coffee and gather her purse, keys and briefcase as she rose to her feet.

"You don't remember me, do you?" he said, and had her easing back down in the chair.

She gave him more than a quick glance and realized it wasn't only the look in his eyes that put her guard up. It was the whole face. "I didn't recognize you at first, Jerry," she said, "but I've never forgotten you."

He sat back in his chair, chest puffed out, smile going just over the line of pleased and into smug.

"I didn't say the memories were pleasant."

He was still smiling, but it was razor-thin, more of a sneer than anything else. "You always thought you were too good for everybody else."

"Not everyone, just you." She picked up her cup, but it was empty, nothing left in it to help her fight off the coldness that washed over her. Jerry's house—or rather his parents' house—had been the one she'd lived in after Mrs. Runion's. Her residence there had been mercifully short, and yet it was without a doubt the worst part of her life. "I should have told them about you."

"Who would've believed it?"

That had been the problem, Emmy remembered. Jerry's parents were nice people, but there'd always been an unspoken line drawn between their only son and the orphans who never quite measured up. Even when he got arrested for shoplifting they'd blamed themselves for indulging him too much.

They'd taken in foster children for a short while after that, in an attempt to… Emmy wasn't quite sure of their reasoning. Maybe they'd hoped having the less fortunate around would make Jerry see his blessings instead of focusing on material possessions. Maybe they thought some latent streak of kindness would show up in a child who'd been taught to think only of himself. Whatever their hopes, they'd been disappointed. Jerry was too lazy to do his own schoolwork, but he was smart enough to bully someone into doing it for him, and when he wanted something his parents wouldn't buy him, he'd pressed his foster siblings into crime. Including Emmy.

Thinking of it still brought back the hopelessness and shame of those few months, the humiliation of being arrested, and the relief at being taken away from Jerry's parents and put in another home. Even if she'd gone into a far worse place, it still would have felt like a reward to be sent away.

"Maybe your parents wouldn't have believed me," Emmy said, "but at least they would have sent me away sooner." She got to her feet.

His hand shot out and closed around her wrist. "Don't you even want to know why I'm here?"

"No," Emmy said, her voice carefully modulated and absolutely rock-steady, even though her insides were quivering. "If you don't get your hand off me I'm going to do two things. First I'll spray you with this." She showed him the pepper spray clipped to her key ring. Her finger was on the trigger. "And then I'm going to scream and make sure you get arrested."

He squeezed, once, until her bones felt as if they were grinding together.

She lifted the spray toward his face and he let her go. "Come near me again and I'll get a restraining order."

"Don't flatter yourself," he said, "I'm only here because

he—" Jerry stopped, sneered out a smile and then continued, "No, I'm not going to tell you that."

He walked off, and Emmy didn't think twice about what he'd left unsaid. She was too happy to see him go.

She headed back into the coffee shop, needing to be around people, but once she was through the door she only stood there, wondering what to do with herself.

"Can I help you?"

She gasped, slapping a hand to her pounding heart as she spun around to goggle at the teenage boy behind the counter.

He jumped back, eyes going wide and startled. "Jeez, lady," he said, "let me get you some coffee."

Emmy could only imagine what her expression must be to make this kid look at her as though he was silently reciting 911 to himself. "Coffee isn't going to do it," she said. "I need chocolate." She eyed the little Bunsen burner under the teapot behind the counter, wondering if it was possible to mainline chocolate.

The kid, Mikey, his nametag said, reached for a glass jar filled with chocolate chip cookies the size of her face. Lots of sugar, hardly any chocolate.

"No. I need chocolate. Actual chocolate."

"We don't sell candy."

"What is that?" Emmy pointed to a second jar, filled with little brown beads.

"Chocolate covered coffee beans," Mikey said.

Coffee and chocolate, why had she never noticed that before? "I'll take them."

"How many?"

Emmy slapped a twenty on the counter. Mikey inched his hand toward it, snatching the bill back so he didn't have to get too close to her, then scooping chocolate-covered coffee beans into a bag.

A young woman came out of the back room, only slightly

older than Mikey but clearly his superior—in attitude if nothing else. "You're not supposed to sell that many of those," she said.

Mikey indicated Emmy with a couple jerks of his head.

The girl looked her way, eyes widening when she got a good look at Emmy's expression. "Yikes," she said and handed her the bag. "Just don't eat too many of them at one time, lady."

"How many is too many?" Emmy wanted to know.

Mikey and the girl traded a glance, each of them doing some version of you-got-me. Apparently no one had ever asked them that question before.

The girl shrugged. "Try to pace yourself."

Chapter Ten

Emmy wasn't sure what "pace yourself" meant, but the trip to Porter and Son took about fifteen minutes, and she'd polished off half the chocolate-covered coffee beans by the time she arrived. She wasn't feeling a thing. Until she got out of the car.

Her head spun when she stood up. She caught hold of the doorframe and stood there while her muscles jumped and her eyeballs vibrated. Nick must've been waiting for her to show up, because he came out to the parking lot, took one look at her and hustled her into his office, shutting the door practically on Stella's nose.

"What's wrong?"

Words tried to tumble out of Emmy's mouth; she popped another coffee bean instead, chewing frantically. She'd come to terms with what she'd done all those years ago, and why, but there was still enough humiliation left over to keep her from talking easily about it. What was more, she didn't want to drag Nick into that time of her life, or drag that time of her life into the present. Nick was fun and bright and he looked at her as if she was fun and bright, and she wasn't going to…to cloud things up with the foster memories, with the unhappiness and the loneliness and the feeling that she didn't belong anywhere. She'd made a life for herself. It wasn't perfect, and it might not include Nick for very much longer, but it was her life and she didn't want to go backward.

"Nothing's wrong," she said.

"Where were you yesterday?"

"Things to do," she said, "lists to make."

"Without this?" He reached behind him, retrieved something from his desk and held it out to her. "You left it in my car."

Emmy took her day planner, realizing just how torn up she must've been not to notice it was missing in the first place. "Thanks."

"Are you grateful enough to tell me what's going on?"

She popped another bean, her mind racing, her feet moving. "I told you, I had a bad day. I...I didn't sleep very well, so I decided to stay home."

"I'm sorry."

"Why? It had nothing to do with you."

Nick didn't look like he was buying it. "It was the charity fair, wasn't it?" he said.

"I had a great time at the fair."

"Not at first. When we first got there you weren't too happy, and then that woman—"

"I was only surprised. Look, I'm wearing the ring." She held her hand up to prove it. "It's turning my finger green, but—"

"That's not it," Nick said.

"It isn't?"

"Nope."

"Fine," Emmy said. He wanted to know what was wrong, she'd tell him. What did it matter anyway? "Did I ever tell you I was a foster child? Of course not. I never tell anyone, well, except for Lindy and she'd keep my secrets to the grave."

"Emmy."

She looked up, realized she was pacing. And talking to herself. Nick was listening, of course, but if she kept forgetting he was there she wouldn't self-edit, and that could be so bad. "My parents died when I was young, like too-early-to-remember-them young. I didn't have any relatives, or maybe none of them wanted me, so I went into foster care.

"You know that woman at the charity fair Saturday? Mrs. Runion? I lived with her for a couple of years, and when she sent me back, I went to stay with Jerry's family for a little while. I was twelve and—"

"Jerry?"

"Oh, right, I ran into him this morning at the coffee shop, and let me tell you, he's even more horrible than he was back then."

"How horrible was he?"

"As foster families go? About a five on a scale from one to ten." Emmy popped another coffee bean and rattled off the story of her few months with Jerry and his family, too nerved up to feel like it was more than a recitation of dry facts.

"They took you in as a lesson to their spoiled-rotten brat of a son?" Nick asked when she was done.

Emmy nodded because she was busy chewing again.

"And he made you shoplift for him?"

More nodding, more chewing.

Nick dropped into a chair, looking sick to his stomach. Emmy had been anticipating at least a little sympathy over her sad, downtrodden childhood. Not getting it put the whole situation in perspective. Maybe her formative years hadn't been ideal, but she hadn't really had it all that bad. Standing there, at that moment, what she'd been through didn't seem half as terrible as seeing how much Nick was put off by her story.

Maybe he thought there was something wrong with her, too, Emmy mused, maybe he thought she deserved not to have any parents... No, that wasn't right. Nick wasn't the kind of man who'd think that sort of thing. There was something wrong with her brain, but she couldn't put her finger on what it was. Nick was talking, and he didn't look... She couldn't actually focus on his face, and she couldn't settle long enough to listen to him, but suddenly he was in her path, taking her by the shoulders and shaking her.

"Don't do that," she said, lifting a hand to her heart.

"What's wrong?"

"Palpitations."

Nick smiled.

"Not because of you." Emmy held out the bag.

He peered in it, then at her. "Chocolate-covered raisins give you heart palpitations?"

"N-not raisins."

Nick leaned over and sniffed. "Chocolate-covered coffee beans? Damn, Emmy, how many of these did you have?"

"I think you're about to find out for yourself."

Nick took one quick look at the green tinge to her complexion and hustled her into the bathroom, wincing when he heard her retching, even though it was the best thing for her. The water ran for a minute or so and then she came back out, looking pale but not quite as shaky.

"I feel better," she said, "still a little keyed-up, but better."

"Um—"

"Don't talk to me." She crossed the office, then again, and once more. "This is all your fault, you know."

Nick backed up until he felt his desk behind him. It was that or fall down because his legs had all but buckled at the idea that Jerry might have told her who'd tipped him off.

"My life was fine, I was happy."

"No, you weren't."

"I thought I was. Roger—"

"Is an idiot."

"He wants me back."

Nick didn't say anything right away. First there was the relief to get through because it turned out she wasn't talking about the foster thing, after all. Then the anger kicked in. "Tell Roger to take a hike."

"He won't listen."

"And?"

"You," she said, whipping around to stab a finger in his direction. "You and those eyes. And that mouth. Stop grinning. This is a serious problem. I can't stop thinking about you during the day and at night—" She whirled around, set to pacing again.

"At night what?"

Emmy shook her head.

Nick held on to his patience, but it wasn't easy. Just when it was getting good, she decided to clam up. And leave. "Who are you running away from, Emmy?"

She stopped halfway to the door, but she didn't turn around. "I'm not running."

"You've been running your entire life. From one foster home to another, from Roger, now from me."

She turned slowly, faced Nick with her head held high. "If Roger hadn't backed out of our wedding, I'd be marrying him in a week or so. And this is a job. I thought I made that clear from the beginning."

"Yeah, sure, nothing personal."

"Exactly," Emmy said.

"Then what was that just now?" Nick wanted to know. "Sounded like a whole lot of personal to me."

"I…I was upset. Running into Mrs. Runion and then Jerry." Emmy walked back to face him across his desk, her steps measured and deliberate, her gaze still level on his. "I'm sorry, it won't happen again."

"That's not what I was getting at." Nick ran a hand through his hair, exasperated. "What's wrong with being personal?"

"It's not why I'm here. This is work, and if you call that running away—"

"It's worse than running away, it's hiding. Dammit Emmy, you're not being honest, with me or yourself. You kissed me Saturday—"

"That was a mistake."

That did it. Calling him a mistake made Nick so angry he couldn't find words to express it. And he didn't need to. Emmy saw it on his face, and she wasn't hanging around for the fallout.

She headed out to the factory floor, laid her briefcase on the receiving table, and tried to work. But her hands were shaking, and it wasn't only the chocolate-covered coffee beans.

"You can't work in this state," Nick said, coming up beside her and snapping her briefcase shut.

She took her case away from him, but she didn't dare look him in the eyes, not while she was feeling so vulnerable and needy. "Then I'll go home."

"You're not driving either."

"The hell I'm not. You can't tell me what to do," she'd already turned toward the door, but she spun around and drilled a finger into his chest, beyond caution. "And you can't tell me how to live my life."

"Emmy…" Nick wrapped his arms around her, and the yearning rose up in her, so quickly she didn't have a prayer of resisting him. "Lean on me, just this once," he whispered against her temple. "Let yourself go."

He pulled back a little, enough to look deeply into her eyes—and unfortunately enough for her to see the entire work force of Porter and Son, frozen at their posts, watching the two of them.

"They don't look very happy," she said, putting some distance between her and Nick.

"I don't give a damn." Nick took a step toward them. They all took a step back.

Emmy spoke up so he didn't do something he'd regret. Their hostility was directed mostly at her, after all. "I suppose this is going to earn me another session with glitter in my umbrella, or something equally original," she said loud enough to reach the farthest edge of their audience. The employees looked like that was exactly what they had on their collective minds. She didn't let it stop her. "If that's all you can come up with, it's no wonder Nick had to hire someone to figure out what's wrong with this place."

The mood of the crowd turned even uglier. She didn't care. What mattered to her was that a few of the workers looked intrigued, and one was concerned enough to pull his head out of the sand and say sullenly, "We didn't know there was anything wrong until the other day."

"Well now you do," Emmy said, "so what are you going to do about it? Sit around thinking up ways to torture me or use all that creativity to come up with some useful suggestions?"

"Don't see why we can't do both," someone else chimed in.

There was laughter, but it wasn't exactly a crowd-wide sentiment. "Mr. Porter is trying to save this company," Emmy announced, "and believe it or not I'm trying to help. Cutting jobs is the last action that should be taken, but if things don't improve that's where you're headed."

The employees milled around, murmuring and seeming uncertain, but at least they weren't looking at her as though she was single-handedly responsible for the end of life as they knew it.

"That was good," Nick said. "They're not all convinced, but at least they're listening. What do we do now?"

"Put up a suggestion box, and see if some of them use it."

"All of them will use it," Nick said, "they just won't make suggestions you'll want to take."

NICK SENT Emmy home in a cab. The employees had gone back to work, and since they seemed to have a lot to think about, thanks to Emmy, Nick decided to leave them alone to get on with it. He had some things to sort through himself, which was a new predicament for a man who preferred to bounce along wherever life took him rather than take a hand in steering his own course. That hadn't changed where he was concerned, but he'd stepped all over Emmy's free will with an ends-justify-the-means attitude that didn't seem so simple anymore.

She'd been on the edge when she left Porter and Son, and it wasn't just the caffeine overdose. He'd shoved her to that edge, Nick admitted, with the arrogant assumption that a couple of faces from the past could erase two decades worth of hurt, of feeling worthless and undeserving. What he'd done instead was send her running again.

Or had he?

Sure, she'd denied she had a problem, but she'd gone on the defensive, too, and didn't that mean that the shell she'd built around herself was beginning to crack? Why else would she be so desperate to hide if the very feelings she'd spent so much of her life shutting out weren't starting to leak through?

And ironically, it was the bad memories that had brought her to that potential breakthrough. Nick had spoken to the families, only asking help from those he'd believed were truly interested in her welfare. Jerry's parents had seemed like wonderful people, and if one of them had come to visit Emmy, the outcome might have been completely different. Instead they'd sent the son they still believed to be perfect. At first Nick had been horrified to know that Emmy had been made to relive one of the worst times in her life; now he could see that it wasn't the good memories that were strong enough to open her up, it was the ones that had sent her into hiding in the first place.

Thank God Emmy was tough, but it wasn't her strength Nick was questioning. It was his own. His first instinct, after Emmy had told him about her encounter with Jerry, had been to stop what he'd started. But if he backed off now, it wouldn't be for her sake. It would be because he couldn't bear to see her hurting. If he backed off now, what she'd already gone through would have been for nothing.

It was going to get even harder, too, because Nick knew he had to keep his distance. On top of everything else, trying to kiss Emmy had been the absolute worst thing he could do, especially in front of everyone at Porter and Son. He couldn't think of anything more certain to send her running for cover. He could be her boss, he could even be her friend. Anything more was out of the question.

He'd been sitting outside her house for about a half hour, coming to terms with the fact that he was going to lose Emmy before she was ever really his, but that was the way it had to be.

There was a knock on the driver's-side window. Nick jumped about a foot, but he was reaching for the door handle almost before he saw who it was.

"What are you doing here?" Emmy asked, stepping back to let him out.

"What are *you* doing here?"

"I went for a run. Trying to work the crazy out of my system." Even as she explained, she did a little boxing jog, just on the tips of her toes, proving she hadn't come all the way down yet.

For once Nick had been too caught up in his own angst to notice what she was wearing. Suddenly he couldn't take his eyes off the tight little shorts and tank, the interesting slide of muscles under her smooth skin, and the even more interesting non-muscular activity.

"I'm fine," Emmy said.

"Huh?"

"I'm fine," she repeated, "if that's what you're here to find out."

Nick shook himself, pulled his gaze up to her face, and remembered why he'd left work in the middle of the afternoon. It was like a cold shower. Okay, more like a cool shower, but it brought him back far enough for his discomfort to turn from physical to mental.

"I was worried about you," he said. "Running into that guy this morning, and the caffeine." *And then me,* he added, silently because the only way he could say it out loud would be jokingly, and what he felt for Emmy was no joke.

Emmy wasn't so clueless as all that. "This isn't about Jerry, or the caffeine," she said. "All right, maybe it is, but not entirely. It's about you, Nick." She went around the back of his car and took the walkway leading up to her house.

Nick followed her. She turned at the door and looked him in the eyes. He felt the impact of that look, right down to his toes. "What about me?" he managed to wheeze out.

She fisted her hand in his shirt, dragged him into the house, and kissed him. She put a lot into that kiss, and he gave as good as he got, crushing her mouth beneath his. One hand banded around her back, the other dropped lower, cupping her bottom so he could press into her heat and softness.

"Now," she said, dropping her mouth to his neck, her hands busy pulling his shirttails loose.

Nick knew she was tired of being alone, knew she saw him as the answer to that, but he'd done a lot of soul-searching in the last few hours, and he was sticking by the decision he'd made. "Emmy," he said, finding the strength from somewhere to take a step back. "I don't think this is a good idea."

Emmy didn't move a muscle, but the light in her eyes died out. "What's wrong?" she said, and Nick knew what she was feeling without needing her to put it in words.

He knew he came off like a man who didn't take life too seriously, and she'd dumped seriously all over him that morning. Emmy thought he was backing off, and he had no choice but to prove her wrong, trapped by his own good intentions. He couldn't tell Emmy the truth, and he couldn't reject her, not when he'd already seen how much it would hurt her.

And not when he'd wanted her from the first moment he'd laid eyes on her.

He took her in his arms. She resisted at first, but he soothed his hands over her back until she relaxed against him. Then he rested his cheek against her soft, ticklish hair, and let everything go but the feel of Emmy in his arms, her hands warm on his sides, her mouth nuzzling his neck....

If they got through this, and Emmy didn't hate him, he'd imagined they'd go on a few actual dates, get to know each other better and eventually they'd get to sex. There'd be music and candlelight and— She stuck her tongue in his ear and he decided they didn't need music or candlelight. They were taking a shortcut and so what? Emmy might be using him to make herself feel wanted and needed, but it was only a starting point; he didn't intend to let her make it a short-term remedy.

She'd been thinking about him, day and night. That was what she'd said. He'd damn well been thinking about her, thinking, fantasizing, crawling out of his skin.

Her hands slipped beneath his shirt, over his bare chest. Her soft touch sent need spearing down. Her fingers followed, settling at his waistband and flipping the button open. He tried to hold on to his thoughts, but she snaked a hand down his pants, closed it around him, and he wondered what was so important about thinking anyway. His thoughts would be there later, he told himself, barely holding on to the presence of mind long enough to make a wild, one-armed swipe at the door to send it crashing closed.

All that mattered was Emmy, laughing breathlessly as she grabbed the hem of her tank and swept it off over her head, her sports bra following. Nick just had time to drop his eyes to small, perfect breasts tipped with rose-pink nipples before she pressed them against his chest. Her eyes were on his as she eased his zipper down, her tongue slipping out to wet her lips and his breath clogged in his lungs.

He struggled to draw in air and then he was fighting gravity because his pants and boxers were down around his ankles and Emmy was laughing again, both hands on his chest, pushing him over. He caught her hips and took her down with him. One elbow rapped hard on the floor, but there was no pain. Nick didn't feel the cold slate tile beneath him, because Emmy was on top of him, burning him alive.

She kissed him again, wild, greedy. He skimmed his hands down her body and discovered she was still wearing her shorts, which didn't fit into his current plans. Emmy must've agreed because she helped him and when they were gone, she straddled him, ran her fingers inside the neck of his shirt and ripped it open. Buttons went flying, one of them catching him on the cheek.

"Ouch," he said although it was more a reflex than a statement of pain.

"Poor baby," she whispered, laying her lips on the spot where the button had struck, and then moving her mouth to his, since it was such a short, convenient distance away.

If she'd been able to reason, she might have wanted to draw this out, make the first time with Nick something incredible that she'd never forget. But there was such a fire in her blood. Her heartbeat was roaring in her ears, and the depth of the need that had been building inside her was nearly immeasurable and completely uncontrollable now that she'd begun to let go.

She wasn't typically this uninhibited about sex, but Nick was lying there, his pants around his ankles, with that smile of his, and those eyes… He was so handsome just seeing him took her breath away, but it was the way he looked at her that never ceased to make her feel beautiful and sexy—and powerful, she realized, feeling strength course through her along with the heat and the desire.

He curled a hand behind her neck. He wasn't smiling anymore and his expression was even hotter, almost frighteningly intense, as he tugged her down beside him. He kissed her, slow and thorough. His hands were on her, shaping her breasts but gently, and that was the last thing she wanted—

"Jeez, Emmy," he said, his voice sounding as though it was being dragged from the soles of his feet. "Don't tell me you're changing your mind."

She realized she was pushing him away.

"I'll stop if you want me to—"

"I don't want you to stop," she said, "I want you to stop being so careful."

He stared at her for a second before it sank in, then he smiled, but this smile had an edge to it. She liked the edge, especially when it got her what she wanted, which was his hands on her, and his mouth, everywhere, at her breasts and center, driving her up and over. The first orgasm ripped through her on wave after wave of pleasure so intense it left her wrung out and gasping for air. Until he touched her again.

When he touched her the need started to build, as strong and stunning as the first time. Again Nick was there, joining their bodies in a long, slow slide that wasn't even close to frenzied enough for her current needs. She wrapped her legs around his waist, braced her hands on his chest and tried to speed up the pace. Nick wouldn't allow it. He twined his fingers with hers, staked her hands to the floor and set a pace that forced her to feel every excruciatingly slow thrust, the slide of his skin, his labored breath washing over her, both hot and cool where her skin was damp from the fevered blood racing beneath.

"Look at me," he said, keeping to the same measured pace, though she could tell from his voice that it was a supreme effort. "Emmy."

She opened her eyes and met his, felt his hands on her, his body stroking hers, and she shot to peak again before she could draw another breath. Nick was there again, gathering her close and letting himself go over with her. And while her body was still humming with aftershocks, he collapsed beside her, cradling her against his side.

Emmy rested her head on his shoulder, draped an arm and a leg over him, and said, "We're on the floor in my entryway."

"Yeah," Nick said.

"We should probably move."

"Yeah," he said again, although neither of them made the effort.

"I don't think I have any bones left," Emmy observed lazily, although it was really her muscles that seemed to be the problem. They'd gone all soft and loose, only a minor quiver now and then that had nothing to do with chocolate-covered coffee beans. Nick had burned the caffeine out of her system.

"We could go into my bedroom," she suggested after another minute.

Nick tipped her chin up and studied her face.

"The floor is starting to get cold," she said, because that was easier than admitting she wanted him to stay with her.

"If we climb into your bed," Nick said, "we're not getting out any time soon."

Chapter Eleven

Emmy woke up in Nick's embrace. She liked it. A lot. She liked it even more when he woke up, too. His arms tightened around her, almost crushingly tight. She didn't mind. He nuzzled her neck and sent shivers coursing over her, and she really didn't mind. He started to pull away. She minded that.

"Where are you going?" she asked.

"We had a pretty energetic night," Nick said. "I thought I'd let you sleep in."

"I feel wonderful," she said, stretching and rubbing a foot over his leg. "Almost perfect."

"Almost?"

Emmy smiled, lifted an eyebrow, and skimmed her fingertips down to his belly. "We never had dinner last night." Right on cue her stomach growled.

"Hey, this was your idea," Nick said.

Some of the playfulness washed away on a slight tide of embarrassment. She leaned back so she could see his face. "Is it all right? That I started things off?"

"Are you kidding? It's every man's fantasy. Feel free to start things off any time you like."

"I have a feeling you're not going to give me many opportunities."

Nick shrugged, but he was grinning, too. "I might lose interest—in fifty or sixty years."

And there went Emmy's desire, nudged aside by the first inkling of panic. "Nick…"

He put a finger over her lips. "I was teasing, and even if I wasn't we don't have to think about that right now. But there is something we should talk about, Emmy, that guy yesterday—"

"I don't want to talk about him."

"I know," Nick said. He'd been over and over his predicament in the long sleepless hours, holding Emmy and thinking about what would be best for her. If he told her the truth now she'd only push him away. She'd be hurt and angry, and instead of something good coming out of her impromptu foster reunions, she'd consider what he'd done just one more example of her dismal failure when it came to interpersonal relationships. If he came clean now it could ruin her for life. And yet it still felt wrong.…

"Nick?"

He gave her a slight, reassuring squeeze, working up a smile to go with it. She settled back into his arms, and he knew he'd made the right decision. And that the guilt he was feeling was the price he had to pay for it.

"I was just thinking that Jerry came back into your life for a reason," he said. "Maybe the time has come for you to face the bad memories from your childhood and put them behind you."

"Do you think it's that simple?"

"Of course not, but—"

"Jerry's family wasn't even the worst placement I had. You learn things in foster care." She threw the sheet back and got out of bed, putting on her robe before Nick had time to be sidetracked. "You learn to judge people fast, and you learn to stay away from the ones who are…trouble."

"I understand that, Emmy."

"No, you don't. You had parents who loved you."

"That's true, but just because I had parents who loved me doesn't mean my childhood was perfect. My dad…"

"What about your dad?" she asked, looking at him for the first time since she'd left the bed.

"I know my father loved me, but he didn't have any faith—" He let the rest of his pent-up breath out in a rush, but the words stayed bottled up inside him. He couldn't bring himself to tell her his own father had believed he'd be a failure, not when that prediction might actually come true. "This isn't about me," he said instead. "You're closed off, Emmy. You never learned how to deal with relationships, just like I don't know anything about efficiency."

"But you can learn about efficiency. Love isn't that simple."

"No, love is a mess sometimes. And it takes a lot of work. Are you afraid to try?"

"Are you saying you love me?"

Yes tried to pop out of his mouth, but he choked it back, not sure where it had come from—not sure it was even *true*. The one thing he was sure of was the terror in Emmy's eyes. He wasn't ready to admit to love, and even if he had been she'd bolt two seconds after hearing it, and he'd never see her again. "I'm saying I feel something for you and I'm willing to find out what it is. And what it could grow into." And since Nick could see he'd pushed her about as far as possible, he kissed her on the forehead and went to take a shower.

She hadn't told him much about her foster-care years, but she'd given him a pretty complete picture of what it must've been like. He didn't have time to dwell on it, though, or regret that he'd even brought it up, before the shower curtain flipped back and Emmy stepped in.

She wrapped her arms around his waist and rested her cheek against his shoulder. "I don't want to fight," she said.

Nick turned and laid his hands on her shoulders, and Emmy felt all the tension drain out of her. The way he kissed helped, too, starting off slow and careful, a deliberate tease that made her sigh and yearn. And then he deepened the kiss and gathered her against him. She closed her eyes and sank in, let her heart race and her head spin until it was blessedly empty of thoughts. And memories.

Nick hooked one of her knees, lifting her leg high up on his hip and slipping inside her, his eyes on hers the whole time. Sensation beat at her, emotion swamped her, the combination so powerful and so overwhelming that she could only brace herself against him and hold on tight. Hot water poured down, steam billowed, and pleasure built. Each caress of Nick's hands, every slide of his body within hers was both agony and ecstasy until she couldn't bear anymore and shattered into a million bits of light and color, an overload of physical joy. Because that's all she would allow it to be.

NICK'S HOUSE was in an older neighborhood of large homes on generous lots shaded by mature trees, comfortably ensconced in the heart of Dorchester, one of Boston's most stable communities. A quietly expensive, upscale, family neighborhood where dads went off to their high-powered jobs, moms stayed home and made cupcakes and meat loaf, and kids rode bikes in the street or played in front yards. Emmy didn't have proof of any of that—except for the kids, since they were clearly visible and engaged in those activities. The rest of it was subject to interpretation. For all she knew the moms were out bringing home the bacon, and the houses were populated by stay-at-home dads and hired nannies. But it looked like the kind of place where the nuclear family and traditional roles would have made Donna Reed and June Cleaver feel right at home.

It didn't take a genius to figure out Nick had grown up in

that house, even before they walked in and Emmy discovered the place was furnished with nostalgia. Family photos hung on the walls, heirlooms filled the china cabinet, and somewhere, Emmy imagined, there was a wall where Nick's mother had carefully measured and made a mark above his head each year on his birthday.

It was exactly the kind of place she'd dreamed of as a child, a home not because of the wood and shingles, but because it was a place to belong.

The doorbell rang, and Nick yelled, "Can you get that?" because he'd gone up to change his clothes, and in the interest of getting to work any time soon Emmy had opted to stay downstairs, out of the hormonal overload danger zone.

She opened the door to find a pair of grubby boys in the under-ten age range and a dog with three legs. "Hello," she said.

"Hi. I'm Justin," the older of the two boys said. "He's James, my brother."

Emmy took the hand he held out, doing the same with his brother, then contemplated the dog. "This must be Tripod."

"How'd you know his name?"

"Nick told me."

"He's not our dog, but he likes to hang with us sometimes, 'specially if we're coming over to Nick's," Justin said.

"Hmm."

James grinned up at her, his two front teeth missing. "He don't bite or nothin'," he said with a slight lisp, rubbing the dog's ears until it collapsed on the ground, tongue lolling, tail wagging, all three feet in the air. James gave his belly a good scratch, looking up at her for approval. Emmy kept her participation to an encouraging smile. She'd grown up in places where dogs weren't always cherished family members and better-safe-than-sorry was the best attitude to have where they were concerned; she'd never quite outgrown the need to keep her distance.

"Nick around?" Justin asked.

Emmy stepped aside, and they trooped in, Tripod scrambling up and doing a strangely endearing shuffle-hop behind the two boys.

"Nick!" Justin yelled.

"Nick!" James echoed, going to the foot of the stairs and peering up into the gloom of the second floor.

Nick, freshly dressed, pounded down the stairs. He had a duffel in one hand and a huge smile on his face. "Hey," he said, dropping the duffel to high-five the boys. "What's up?"

"Mom sent us over to tell you she's making pot roast and you're invited."

"We get to eat on the new table," James chimed in.

"Man, pot roast and the new table." Nick grimaced, rubbing at the back of his neck. "I can't make it tonight, guys. Tell your mom I'm sorry."

"Why?" Justin wanted to know.

"I have a date."

"With her?"

"Yep."

Justin shrugged. "She can come too. Mom was gonna toss another potato in the pot for you. I guess she can toss in two."

Nick looked at Emmy, trying not to grin. "You like potatoes, Emmy?"

"Potatoes…um, sure, but…I have, um, other plans."

Nick's eyes took on a speculative glint, one brow inching up to give his smile a suggestive smirk. Clearly Nick thought he was the "other plans." Emmy frowned and shook her head slightly. Not that she didn't want to have sex with Nick, she just didn't want him to read more into it. They'd only been together for one day; it was too soon to be meeting his neighbors and fitting herself into his life.

"Sorry guys," he said to Justin and James, scooting them

toward the still-open door, "we'll have to take a rain check." The second they were gone, he turned to Emmy. "What's wrong?"

"You didn't ask me out, for one thing."

"So you think I'm taking it for granted that we're going to be together."

She stared pointedly at the duffel.

Nick ignored her inference. "You're a little freaked out about the whole family-home thing. And you want to take it slower."

"Well…yeah."

"And now you're irritated because I'm right."

"Have you been watching Oprah? Reading *Men are from Mars, Women are from Venus?* Getting in touch with your feminine side?"

Nick crossed his arms.

"Fine," Emmy huffed, "I need to take it slower."

"Then we'll take it slower." He curled his hand around hers and stooped to gather up his duffel, but he straightened again without it. "Does that mean I'm not the 'other plans?'"

"No, just…" Emmy gestured around her, "I'm not ready for this."

"Jeez, I haven't even asked you out yet and you already want to move in with me? Slow down, okay?"

Emmy laughed, but she wasn't fooled. Nick might be taking it slow verbally, but that didn't mean the intense way he looked at her hadn't taken on a dimension of hunger since last night. It would be flattering to be wanted so much, if it wasn't so damned scary.

At the moment, though, she had other things to worry about; namely showing up late at Porter and Son, and in the same car with Nick. Sure, he'd changed his clothes, and Emmy was careful to keep her distance on the walk from the parking lot to the office. But they weren't fooling anyone.

The workers were gathered in the big bay door of the factory, watching as Nick pulled into his parking space. Stella had her nose pressed to the office window. Clearly, Emmy concluded, she was still Public Enemy Number One.

"I should have driven myself," she said to Nick.

"No point in taking two cars when we're going to the same place," he replied, his voice teasing. "An efficiency expert should know that."

And she hadn't wanted to hurt Nick's feelings. She knew he was feeling the emotional distance she'd put between them; she hadn't wanted to upset him more by refusing to get in the same car with him. There still had to be boundaries, though.

She followed Nick to the office door, keeping one eye on his employees. "I think it's best if we keep a professional relationship when we're working."

"Darn," Nick said, "I had plans for my desk."

Emmy rolled her eyes, but she couldn't quite keep the smile from her face. Nick's eyes dropped to her mouth, lingered, his gaze a caress that shot her from business mode to personal so fast she had to look away before she broke all her own rules.

To make matters worse, Nick's employees weren't missing a thing. Maybe they'd gathered because they felt bad about yesterday, maybe they even wanted to apologize. Emmy caught the knowing looks passing between them and realized that whatever ground she'd gained was lost. They might have decided they could go along with her newfangled ideas long enough to see the back of her walking away for good. Her getting personally involved with the boss was another story.

Stella had been prepared for the possibility since day one, and she was ready with the evil eye when Emmy followed Nick through the office door. "You missed lunch with a supplier yesterday," she said. "I called your cell phone. You didn't answer." Her gaze shifted back to Emmy. "Or return my messages."

"The supplier can reschedule. Let's go put together that suggestion box," he said to Emmy.

She knew he was only using it as an excuse, but he'd been so reluctant to make any real, substantial changes, that she wasn't above taking advantage of it. She had come to help him save his company, after all. That hadn't changed just because she'd crossed a personal line.

"A cardboard box works pretty well," she said as soon as he closed the office door behind them, "but you can use anything from a large brown envelope to a file folder."

Nick's arms came around her. "I have a few suggestions of my own."

"I'm being serious." Emmy slipped out of his arms and set her briefcase on his desk.

"They won't take it seriously," Nick said, "but we can try."

Emmy could see he was only humoring her, but that was all right, too.

"Cardboard isn't going to cut it," he said.

He led her out to the small workshop off one side of the big factory floor, gathered up some scraps of wood, and a hammer and nails. Over the course of a half hour he cobbled together a rectangular box about twice the size of a tissue container. It had the requisite slot in the top, and the back was a couple of inches bigger than the front, all the way around, with a good-sized hole drilled in each of the four corners. The holes were a mystery until Nick gathered up a length of chain and a padlock, took the box into the work area, and bolted it to a pillar.

"Is that really necessary?"

"Yes," Nick said. "Trust me, I know these people."

"They don't look as open-minded as they did yesterday," Emmy conceded.

"That was yesterday. Either they've had time to get over

it, or the rest of them ganged up on the weaklings and convinced them to stick to their guns."

"I don't think they'd pull out actual guns, but tar and feathers might top the list of possibilities." Emmy took a closer look into the factory and jammed her hands on her hips. "Dammit," she hissed, "they moved the production lines back to their old configuration."

Nick looked, too, and then he laughed. "You're right. I didn't notice it when we first came out here."

Neither had she because she'd been too busy trying to act as if nothing had changed, which hinged a great deal on not making eye contact with people who were searching for any little clue that things had, indeed, changed.

Nick went over to Marty Henshaw, foreman on line one, and asked a question that presumably went along the lines of "Why did you change the production lines back?"

Emmy didn't have any trouble hearing the response.

"She told us to take responsibility for this place," Henshaw said. "We think the way we've been doing things for thirty years is good enough, so we took responsibility and changed it back."

"Sound familiar?" Emmy asked Nick once he'd rejoined her.

Nick rolled his eyes.

Emmy found that reaction irritating. "It's your company," she said. "I'm here to make suggestions, not to force you to implement them."

"They're trying," Nick said.

"Do you really think they'd have done this if they weren't sure there'd be no repercussions?"

"What's that supposed to mean?"

"I don't think it requires an explanation."

Nick caught her arm before she could walk away.

She looked at his hand, then at their audience. "I have an appointment," she said coolly, "I need my car."

"Don't pull back, Emmy. Tell me what you meant."

"I'm here to advise you on your business, not your employees. Or your personal life."

"Last night was pretty personal."

"Last night was just last night." When she saw his expression, she said, "No, don't get angry." She couldn't explain that when she said *personal* she meant what he'd said that morning, about his father. After seeing how upset he'd been, she wasn't prepared to delve into a subject she knew would only cause an argument. Unfortunately, the diversion she'd chosen was just as emotionally charged. "Neither of us knows where this is going, Nick. Don't you think it's a bit soon for me to be picking apart your life and making helpful suggestions about how you can improve yourself?"

Nick shrugged. "If you picked apart my life and made helpful suggestions I'd probably just ignore them. I'm pretty stubborn."

"I've noticed," Emmy said. "Now, I need my car."

"But—"

"It's not about this…difference of opinion. I told you, I have a lunch." She went back into the office, took out her planner and handed it to him, opened to the day.

Nick barely glanced at it. He already knew what was in there; since she'd left it so conveniently in his car, he'd peeked at the next couple of weeks so that when he'd contacted her foster families he'd been able to give them places and times to "run into" her.

Emmy held out her hand and he put the book in it.

"I'll take your car keys, too."

"No."

"Then I'll have to call a cab." Emmy pulled out her cell phone. Nick plucked it from her hand and snapped it closed.

"I'll drive you."

"Really, Nick, that's nice of you, but I'm meeting with a new client."

That stopped him for a minute, and Emmy didn't miss his reaction. "I'm nearly done here," she said, "but I'm not done paying my mortgage."

Nick had never considered the possibility she'd move on personally and somehow that had translated into professionally as well. But he had to protect her. He'd made the decision not to call off her foster families, but he intended to be around if or when any of them showed up. "I'll take you," he said again.

Emmy took a step back, her face twisted into a little, bemused frown. "No offense, Nick, but it will seem kind of strange for me to have my current client at a meeting for a new one."

"I can give you a recommendation."

"Personally or professionally?"

Nick slipped his hands in his pockets and rocked back on his heels. But he was smiling. "I'll take you anyway, and then I'll find something to do with myself while you're having lunch. Maybe I'll go pack enough for the rest of the week, instead of just one night."

Emmy felt her cheeks heat, but she didn't avoid his eyes, and she didn't contradict his assumptions.

Nick smiled full-out, the smile that always lit her up on the inside, and she was glad she hadn't talked her way into an argument with him. Spending the next few days in Nick's arms was worth more than banishing the red ink from his company books, more even than finishing one of her famous lists. For once in her life she wasn't going to think of consequences.

If she was lucky, she wouldn't be thinking much at all.

Chapter Twelve

Nick was waiting in front of the restaurant where Emmy had had lunch, narrowing his eyes as she came out—but not in her direction. He didn't like the way her lunch date was looking at her, or the way he leaned in, lingering over the handshake. Nick didn't like the man's face either; he had the kind of face women tended to appreciate, and he was using it to smile at Emmy.

"So?" he asked when she'd given the man a firm, professionally brief handshake, and walked away from him.

"What?" She stopped a couple of steps from Nick, frowning up at him. "Something wrong?"

She looked so wary that he couldn't impose his jealousy on her, and anyway, it wasn't Emmy's professionalism he was questioning, it was her client's. "No, just wondering how the lunch went."

"Good," she said, "really good. Marcus—"

"Marcus?"

Emmy sent him a look. "The client is definitely excited about my ideas."

"I saw," Nick replied, although it wasn't Emmy's ideas the man had had his eyes on.

"He was even excited about some of the changes I suggested—or I should say hinted at. I didn't want to give it all away before he hired me."

Nick knew she was half teasing. It was the other half that got to him. "Change isn't always the solution."

"Yes, it is." Emmy put a hand on his arm and, waited until he met her eyes. "There's no treading water, Nick. Either you're growing or you're going."

"Emily!"

She kept walking, but she turned her head to search the crowd behind them. Nick slung an arm around her shoulder and steered her down the sidewalk in the direction they'd been headed.

"I thought I heard somebody call my name," Emmy said, glancing over her shoulder again.

"You've been working too hard. You're starting to hear things."

Emmy laughed softly, but more importantly she faced forward again. "You sound like Lindy. She's always telling me to take time off."

"That's not a bad idea." Nick beeped the car open and put her in the passenger seat, keeping one eye on the post-lunchtime crowd just in case. He didn't relax until he was behind the wheel and they were moving. "I think you should take some time off. In fact, I think you should take the rest of the week off."

"What about Porter and Son? Your employees have undone all my work. I don't think this is the best moment to disappear."

"When's the last time you took a vacation?"

"Yesterday."

"I'm not talking about one day, especially a day you spent thinking about work and making lists."

"What's wrong with making lists?"

"What's wrong with spontaneity?" he countered.

"Most people don't function that way."

"And that makes me wrong and you right?"

She crossed her arms and sat back in her seat. "I'm only trying to help," she said with a bit of a snap to her voice. "That's why you hired me." Her gaze was trained out the passenger window, but her body language spoke volumes. She was offended and hurt, and she had every right to be.

He had hired her, after all. Sure, his banker had doom-and-gloomed him into it, and sure he knew she was an efficiency expert. Even if he'd been taken in by her looks, he understood that a person in her line of work would have…certain personality traits. Somehow, though, he kept forgetting how rigidly controlled she was under all that soft blond hair and smooth white skin.

Despite his initial resistance, he was more than happy to listen to Emmy's ideas on how to get the business back on track—his old man's track. Streamlining was one thing, making changes something else entirely. Changing Porter and Son in order to make it successful would be just as much a failure as going bankrupt. He'd not only prove that he could run the company, he'd prove he could do it better than his father. Anything else would be unacceptable. He'd play by the same rules or he wouldn't play at all.

It wasn't reasonable, somewhere in his own mind Nick understood that. But reasonable wasn't something he could be where his father was concerned. There'd been too much guilt for too long, too much feeling like a failure, too much trying to live up to a legacy on the legacy's terms. And, as always, the weight of the burden and his own stubborn determination to shoulder it made Nick's head hurt. So he went with his own personal mantra; don't deal with the problem until absolutely necessary.

"I don't want to think about work anymore," he said, reaching over to curl his hand around hers.

"It won't go away."

"Exactly. It'll still be there if we take a few days off. The rest of the week. I promise I'll be all business on Monday."

"Nick…"

"Aren't you tired of working all the time?"

Emmy didn't say anything, but her hand tightened on his.

"Maybe we could relax. Together."

She smiled over at him. "I was planning to work in the office this afternoon, and then tomorrow—"

Nick missed the rest of her comment, busy frowning over the first part. "The office?"

"You wanted the office reorganized. It's in the contract."

Right, but that had been before Stella took such an intense dislike to Emmy. "I'm behind you one hundred percent," Nick said, "or I will be on Monday. Take the rest of the week off with me, Emmy. We'll start fresh next week."

She was actually considering it. She almost agreed before reality set in, and she wasn't just talking about the need to keep her personal boundaries intact. "I'm not all that anxious to take on Stella, so I should say yes." This astounded her. She couldn't have imagined taking all that time off. Before Nick.

"But?" he prompted.

"If I don't go back, they'll think they've run me off for good."

Nick set his jaw.

"I'll tell you what," she said, partly to stop him from getting himself in a mood, partly because it was so tempting. "When I'm done with the office, and I feel like I've made some progress with the rest of your employees, we'll take a few days off, together."

Nick thought it over, and decided after the poor way Stella had treated Emmy, she deserved to have Emmy let loose on her. "Deal," he said. "You get the office straightened out, I'll get the lines put back to their new configuration—"

"No, Nick, if you make them do it, they'll just resent me more, and it won't solve anything. I have to find a way to convince them."

He groaned. "That may take forever."

"It won't," Emmy insisted with as much confidence as she could muster, "and anyway until then we have the evenings."

"Fine," Nick said, "but when we take time off, I get to decide where."

IT DIDN'T take long—especially with Stella dogging her steps—for Emmy to discover the office was pretty well organized. It was a huge relief, to say the least. Having to convince Stella she needed to change things was a task Emmy just wasn't up to, not with the rest of the employees still playing *Mutiny on the Bounty*.

"Well," she said to Stella, "you could use some updating, maybe do a little more of the accounting on computer."

"Our CPA—"

Emmy held up a hand, then talked over the older woman. "If business picks up you'll have to do more automating, but at the present level the manual method is fine."

Stella's indignation started to ramp down. Suspicion took its place.

"I'm not just saying this so you'll like me," Emmy said. "Anyway, I'll be gone soon and it won't matter."

"If you were planning to run off the minute the contract is ended, you shouldn't have started sleeping with him."

There was a moment of buzzing disbelief in Emmy's head that left her speechless, then anger took hold. "That's really none of your business."

"Like hell it's not." Stella clapped a hand over her mouth. "Now you've made me curse. He loves you," she snapped, "and you're telling me that doesn't mean anything to you?"

Emmy balked a little bit over the part where Nick loved her, but she figured Stella was just being dramatic and went with the far bigger reaction she was having. Puzzlement. "Have I stumbled into an alternative reality? Aren't you the woman who's been trying to get rid of me, oh, since the first time we met?"

"It didn't work, did it?"

"Well, no, because Nick wouldn't… He wants to turn Porter and Son around. It has nothing to do with me."

"Humph," Stella grunted. "Just admit that you're in love with him."

Emmy had to sit down. "I feel like I've crossed into the twilight zone. I'm going out there," she said, pointing to the factory doorway, "where everything is normal and people still hate me."

Stella folded her hands, her mouth went prim—and her eyes fired, giving the lie to her mild body language. "No one hates you."

"You certainly hate my profession, and what I came here to do."

"Porter and Son is fine being run the way Nick's father ran it."

"If that was true, you wouldn't be losing money."

Stella set her jaw. "He doesn't need you."

It came to Emmy like a lightbulb clicking on. "You're insulted that Nick hired me. I'm stepping on your toes."

"You're stepping on everyone's toes. People don't like change, especially when it's a stranger telling them they've been doing things wrong all these years, and they're dragging the company into bankruptcy."

"I told you, it has nothing to do with them. Or you. Or Nick—well, not if he decides to let me do my job."

"You have your work cut out for you, I'll say that much.

Especially since you're your own worst enemy. I'm sorry to be so blunt—"

"No, you're not."

That got a reluctant smile from Stella, but it didn't stop her. "You may be very good at what you do, but frankly you could use some work on your interpersonal skills."

"I know I'm not good with people, but they start off resenting me, and I've found it's better just to do my job and get out as quickly as I can, let the owners soothe the hurt feelings."

"Hogwash. Of course they resent you, but you could win them over. If you wanted to."

"What's that supposed to mean?"

"You're standoffish—oh, I know that was tactless, but it's also true. You don't let people close to you. I don't know the reason. I'd imagine it's because you were hurt somewhere along the line, and I'm sorry for it. But your life would be a lot easier, and fuller, if you opened up a little and let people in."

Emmy let out her pent-up breath, giving herself a moment. She was having a hard time taking all this in. But she wasn't so fuddled that she couldn't see an opportunity when it jumped up and slapped her in the face. "You know I'm just trying to help, right?"

"I can't say I'm thrilled with the way you've gone about it, but yes, I believe you're trying to help."

"You've told me why Nick's employees are so resistant, maybe you can tell me why Nick is."

Stella puffed out her chest and folded her hands, ready to go into non-gossip mode.

"I only want to help. Nick hired me—"

"And he's been completely cooperative." *And then some*, her tone said, the disapproval back full force.

"As long as I stick with improving efficiency, he's fine, but every time I talk about new products he changes the subject, or digs in his heels. Why?"

"I…I can't tell you that. It's just not right. Nick knows what he's doing. Mr. Porter, Senior—"

Emmy tossed her hands up, then got to her feet when that didn't satisfy her frustration. "What is it about the man that everyone is afraid of? Do you really think he'd be so stubborn that he'd let the company fail just so it's run his way?"

"You didn't know him," Stella said. "He was one of those old-fashioned, hard-core businessmen."

"He ran a joke shop," Emmy pointed out. "Didn't he have a sense of humor?"

"Not when it came to Porter and Son. It didn't really matter to him what he manufactured, it was about making money, and he did that very well. There was a time this company was the top of its kind in the nation. It was starting to change before he died. Kids these days want video games and Ipods, not good simple fun."

"Exactly! Times are different. If this company doesn't adjust to suit them it's not going to be around much longer."

Stella leaned forward. "You really think it's that bad?"

"Yes."

It took Nick's secretary yet another minute to work herself around the talking-out-of-school mode. Emmy swallowed her frustration and gave her the time, because she respected the woman's loyalty. And because she knew Stella wanted to help Nick more than she felt the necessity of keeping his secrets.

"Mr. Porter, Senior, was…a difficult man," Stella finally began. "When Nick was little, he had a wonderful relationship with his father. Mr. Porter never let a school event go by without being there to support Nick, no matter what. But once Nick's mother died, well, Mr. Porter still made all the school events, but he was different. Nothing mattered but winning. I think, once it was just him, he felt the weight of parenthood. He was a man who demanded excellence from himself, and he never understood that Nick has a more easygoing nature, not that he doesn't want the best for himself and those around him, mind you. It's just that he has another way of getting there."

Emmy tried, but she just wasn't getting from point A to point B. "I don't really get it."

"Because that's not the end of the story," Stella said. "They had a terrible argument, Mr. Porter and Nick. Mr. Porter had his mind made up that Nick would take over the business. Nick wasn't against that, but he wanted his father to let him run the manufacturing end of the business differently, give the employees more responsibility instead of breathing down their necks all the time. Mr. Porter...Mr. Porter said Nick didn't have the stomach to run this place the way it needed to be run in order to make money. He said Nick wanted to make changes to hide his lack of leadership. And Nick walked away."

"That's how Nick does things," Emmy said. "He must've finished the conversation later, when they could both be calm and rational."

Stella shook her head. "He died. Nick's father. Heart attack. Right in there, after hours. Nobody was here to call an ambulance."

The fact that it took Stella a full minute and a lot of personal turmoil to get that out confirmed Emmy's suspicions. Stella had been in love with Nick's father—Mr. Porter, Senior, as she called him. She would have stepped in after Nick's mother died, if Nick's father had opened his eyes and recognized the possibilities right under his nose.

Emmy put her arm around the older woman and steered

her to a chair. "I'm so sorry," she said, stopping there because any other expression of sympathy would have been an imposition. Whatever she'd assumed, Stella hadn't confided her feelings, and Emmy wasn't going to trespass on the basis of her own assumptions.

Stella waved her off, blew her nose and took a sip of cold tea from the cup on her desk. "To tell you the truth," she said, sounding largely restored, "I doubt Nick would have taken over the company if it hadn't been for guilt. He left his father here, alone, and…"

"And he feels responsible."

"He's that kind of person."

Well that explained a lot. Emmy swiped her hands through her hair, knew she'd left it looking wilder than usual, but she didn't care. She was in a hell of a spot. She understood now why Nick was so set against making changes, and she knew that if he didn't, Porter and Son would fold. And he'd never forgive himself.

If she accomplished what she wanted to accomplish, it was a pretty sure bet Nick would never want to see her again, professionally or personally. On the bright side, it wouldn't be very hard to keep her boundaries intact that way.

Chapter Thirteen

Nick was having an in-depth conversation with his shipping clerk when Emmy came out to the factory floor. He took one look at her, and knew she was riding high on whatever had happened between her and Stella. At first he thought it was anger; she marched right out to the middle of the manufacturing area, jammed her hands on her hips, and took stock of what was going on. A woman with a mission.

That mission, apparently, was Marty Henshaw, and when she turned so Nick could see her face, he realized the force driving her wasn't anger. She was smiling, glowing really. Nick had stayed out of the office on purpose. Sure, his decision had been more along the lines of not getting caught in the middle and becoming collateral damage. But now he wished he'd been there when Emmy took on Stella. Emmy had obviously turned a corner of some sort.

She collared Marty, or rather curled her hand around his arm, and towed him down the line, talking a mile a minute and gesturing. Explaining why she'd changed the lines, Nick decided, telling him why her configuration was better than the one they'd used for thirty years. Marty appeared to be getting it, too, in no small part because Emmy was on fire. Her clipboard was nowhere in sight, and when Marty spoke she listened, laughing, bright-eyed, attentive. The woman Nick had fallen in love with at first sight...

It should have floored him, how simple and easy that thought had slid into his conscious mind and how right it felt to admit it to himself. But he knew he'd been toast the minute he laid eyes on her.

Henshaw was certainly no match for her. No man would be, Nick thought, and struggled not to be jealous.

When Emmy was done talking she stepped back. Marty stayed where he was, scratching his head and fielding looks from the other employees. Nick was on pins and needles with the rest of them. Emmy had clearly put the decision in Marty's hands, and there was really only one way he could go.

"Aw, hell," he said into the silence that had fallen, "the line did work better the other way."

Grinning, Nick walked over to join Emmy. "Did what I think happen really just happen?"

She smiled over at him, looking very satisfied with herself. "If you think I put Marty on the spot and made him justify why his way was better, you're right."

"And he did what you wanted him to do two weeks ago."

"Not because I told him it was necessary and not out of guilt."

Nick frowned. "Am I supposed to understand that?"

"No, I think it will take something a lot more drastic for you to wake up."

Like a psychiatrist, her expression said.

Nick chose not to push the point. Neither did Emmy.

"The important thing is," she said, "since it's his choice, Marty will make sure everyone else gets behind it."

There was an undercurrent to the conversation that Nick wasn't quite getting. But he was pretty sure Emmy had no intention of explaining anything more to him. The fact that she walked away from him was his first clue. She was headed for the suggestion box they'd put up, but Marty Henshaw raced by her, putting himself between her and it.

"It looks like somebody tried to light it on fire," Emmy said.

"We put it out," Marty replied, shifting sideways to block her when she tried to move around him. His eyes darted to Nick, then back to Emmy again.

"You people could use some anger management classes." She tried to nudge Marty aside, but he wasn't budging.

"Um, I think you should wait to read those," Marty said. "Or not read them at all."

Nick surveyed the rest of Porter and Son's employees. Nobody was laughing, or smirking even. There was some nervous fidgeting, but since it was their ringleader changing sides they weren't exactly sure what to do. And more than one of them looked worried.

Marty solved the problem by reaching over, taking the key from Emmy's hand, and unlocking the box. Then he proceeded to take out the papers, cards and assorted flotsam, including something that looked suspiciously like a dead mouse, and stuff the whole mess into his pocket. "Trust me," he said, "you don't want to know what's in there."

"There might be some good suggestions," Emmy pointed out.

"Whoever made them can make them again."

Emmy took a minute, then said, "Okay." She took the key from him and rejoined Nick.

"So," he said, "I'd ask you what happened between you and Stella, but I'm not sure I want to know."

"I wouldn't tell you anyway, and neither would she." She sighed and shook her head a slightly. "It shouldn't have taken so long for me to figure it out."

"I don't imagine you've come up against this amount of stubbornness all in one place before."

"Are you talking about you or them?" she teased.

At least Nick thought she was teasing. "So what now? Going in for the killing shot?"

She looked over at him, sobering because he was the killing shot, and she didn't have the willpower to fire it just yet. Because when she fired it, she would be the one taking the hit.

She'd dealt with Stella, and she'd handled the factory workers. Nick was the only one left who hadn't gotten with the program yet. Judging by the way he'd reacted in the past when she even came close to commenting on his management style, he wasn't going to like what she had to say about the way he was running Porter and Son. He was going to let her know it. And she was going to stick to her guns.

In her life, there'd been so little of what she'd found with Nick. They'd only had one short night together, and she wasn't ready to give him up yet.

"Now that I've made some progress, how about we take the rest of the week off?" she suggested.

"Are you sure?"

"Yes," Emmy said. "I should give your employees some space. Marty will spread the word and they'll all need to think about it. And since I don't have another client yet…"

Nick grabbed her hand and all but dragged her into the office. She collected her briefcase, he told Stella he'd be gone the rest of the week, and Porter and Son was history, at least for a little while.

It didn't stop there. Now that he'd convinced her, sort of, to take some time off work, he planned to make the most of it—starting with home court advantage. "I had some time to think while you were having lunch," he said, "and I thought it might be nice if you spent the night at my house."

She crossed her arms, stared out the windshield, and Nick let her mull it over in total silence. "I don't know, Nick… I wasn't expecting… I'd be more comfortable at my house."

He knew that, which was why he'd decided to bring her to his home. And okay, he wanted to reduce the possibility of running into any more foster people. But he'd been paying attention to the way she dealt with Marty and the rest of his employees. It had to be her decision, and if she agreed to stay with him of her own free will, she'd be more inclined to make the best of it.

"You took a big step with my employees, Emmy. Take a chance on yourself." He took her hand, lifted it and kissed her fingers. "Take a chance on us."

She didn't say anything, just squeezed his hand and settled back into her seat.

Nick felt the urge to pump his fist into the air, but since he was driving with one hand and holding on to Emmy with the other, he had to settle for grinning like a lunatic. That was before he remembered his heart was at stake, and a lifetime with Emmy was on the line.

He only had five nights and four days of uninterrupted time with her, and a laundry list of things he needed to accomplish. Convince her she'd done enough at Porter and Son, make sure she didn't run into any more people he'd let loose on her, get her to fall in love with him.

While he was at it, he thought with a mental eye-roll for his own arrogance, he might as well add Discover the Meaning of Life to his list. It would be as attainable as any of the other items. Maybe more so.

EMMY GOT out of the car and stood in the driveway for a minute, trying not to feel as if she'd landed on another continent, one where she didn't speak the language, didn't know the customs, and where all the natives recognized her instantly as someone who didn't belong there.

Nick held out his hand, and when she put hers in it, said, "Let's go for a walk."

She let Nick thread his fingers between hers, and strolled along beside him, shoulders bumping, chin up, trying not to feel like an alien. Every now and again Nick nodded or lifted a hand to acknowledge a neighbor's wave. He didn't seem to feel the need to talk, and he didn't urge Emmy to talk, or nod or wave.

After a couple of blocks she began to relax a little. She'd made a conscious choice to come here. True, Nick had put her in a position where she couldn't do anything else, but hadn't she been saying the same thing to herself since the moment they'd met? Wasn't this, on some level, what she wanted?

She wasn't ready to examine the reasons she'd chosen to let her guard down with Nick, but one thing was crystal-clear. He wouldn't let her hide, from him or herself. She'd known that from day one, known that if she didn't cancel Nick's contract they'd come to this point. She'd made her choice that day, and when she looked at the big picture, everything in her life had been leading her here, even getting dumped by Roger. Especially getting dumped by Roger.

She had no idea where she and Nick might end up— probably on opposite sides of the city, avoiding each other like the plague—but she owed it to herself to make an effort to learn some things while she had the opportunity.

Stella had filled in some of the blanks, but Nick was still so much of a mystery to her. And she knew if she didn't change, didn't deal with what had made her the woman she was and clean out the toxic parts, she'd end up alone. Or with another Roger.

That didn't mean it was going to be easy. Or that she'd be successful. But she knew the first step was being brutally honest with herself.

This neighborhood, for instance. Sure, it was a big contrast to her life, but she'd chosen to live where she did for reasons that were painfully obvious now. Her house was in an area of new construction, populated by young professionals, locked up, buttoned down, scheduled and regimented to within an inch of their lives. Where there were marriages, there were two incomes, and where there were babies, there were For Sale signs. Recreational areas consisted of tennis courts, a nine-hole golf course, and jogging paths for those who preferred outdoor exercise to a gym in the warm months.

There was nothing like the park they came to when they rounded the corner of Nick's block. It was chock-full of people, dads and kids and dogs, not too many women but it was early evening, and Emmy's original assessment of the neighborhood seemed to be dead on. The men were home from work and on kid and pet detail while the moms played June Cleaver.

The dogs were in a small fenced enclosure, sniffing each other, playing, lolling in the shade with their tongues hanging out. The kids played on swings or slides, plastic climbers in bright colors, or ducks on big springs that let them sway back and forth, while their fathers pushed or caught or watched indulgently. And they all knew Nick, judging by the waves and shouts and the frantic barking of the dogs when he passed by.

He and Emmy stayed on the side of the street opposite the park, but she still had the urge to run screaming until she was back where she belonged. "Everyone's staring at me," she said to Nick.

"They think you're cute," he said.

"They think I'm a freak."

He chuckled. "They're not used to seeing me with a girl-friend."

That jolted Emmy a little. *Girlfriend,* wasn't a word she'd ever used to refer to herself—heck, *fiancée* wasn't a word she'd used, and there was no getting around the fact that she'd been one of those not too long ago. She looked down at her ring finger, and felt the cool rush of relief at finding it naked. She made a point of not looking at her right hand, where Nick's carnival ring was turning her pinkie interesting shades of green. Thinking of it didn't seem to bother her, though, so maybe she wasn't the huge commitment-phobe she thought. And since Roger hadn't been able to hold on to his next relationship it was easy to pin the blame on him.

"I think it's our clothes," Nick said before she let herself wander too far into Roger territory. "We're still dressed for work, and everyone else is wearing shorts."

"I'm dressed for work," Emmy corrected him. And now that she thought about it, Nick was right. She was wearing a skirt and blouse, open at the throat with a lace camisole beneath. The only way she could have looked more out of place was if she'd brought along the jacket that went with her skirt.

But that was only appearances. She felt out of place, too, and that was something she'd have to change. If she had the courage.

"I'll need to go home and get some things," she said, deciding the surface was a good place to start. And once she looked like someone who fitted in, she'd start working on feeling it, too. With Nick's help, she thought she might just get there.

Chapter Fourteen

"Put that away," Emmy said from the depths of her walk-in closet.

"I think I hit the jackpot," Nick said, holding up one of the delicate little whatchamacallits she wore under her blouses or suit jackets, the ones that gave just a tempting peek of lace or silk. "Just so you know, I'm packing everything in this drawer."

Emmy came out of the closet, but before she could take most of her lingerie out of her suitcase and put it back in the drawer, the doorbell rang.

"Saved by the bell," Nick muttered, following her to the front door.

She looked through the peephole and said something that sounded vile under her breath.

It shocked Nick, more because of the anger on her face than anything else. His mind set to racing a mile a minute, searching for a way to keep her from talking to whoever was on her front step. She saved him the problem of finding an answer.

"Do not open that door!" she said to him, disappearing into the bedroom again.

Nick waited until she was out of sight and did exactly what she'd told him not to do. If he was lucky, he could get rid of the problem before she came back with whatever weapon she'd gone to fetch.

A man stood on Emmy's front walk, medium height, medium coloring, forgettable features, expression tuned to pleasant blankness—until he saw Nick. Then his eyes narrowed and the fingers of one hand curled just slightly, heading for a fist before he thought better of it.

"You need to leave, Joe," Nick said to him. "I know I called you—"

"Who?" the guy asked. He tried to brush past Nick.

Nick crowded him back, one hand on the doorknob, blocking the opening with his body. "You're not Joe Esterhaus?"

"No," he said, distracted, on his toes and trying to peer over Nick's shoulder into Emmy's entryway.

"Pete Hannigan?"

"Who's Pete Hannigan?"

"Who the hell are you?"

"Roger. Roger Barnett. Emily!" he yelled.

"Roger?" she called back from the depths of the house. "Just a minute."

She came to the door but Nick wouldn't let her by. "I asked you not to open the door," she said quietly to him. "But you did, so you need to step away and let me deal with this."

He looked back at her, then at Roger, and didn't budge.

"Trust me."

A muscle knotted in his jaw, and it took him a moment to work his way around to it, but finally he opened the door wider. He stood his ground in front of Roger, but he made room for her to stand beside him. And he put his arm around her shoulders, just to make sure Roger got the message.

Unfortunately, Roger wasn't that observant. Or intelligent, apparently.

"Who's this guy?" he asked Emmy.

Emmy was speechless for a second, searching for the right terminology to describe Nick.

"I'm a client," Nick said.

"Why is he holding that?"

Emmy glanced down and realized Nick had a one of her lace camisoles in his hand. "He's more than a client, Roger. Could you give us a minute?" she asked Nick.

He wasn't too happy about it, but he did as she asked, sending Roger a visual warning before he left.

"You moved on pretty fast," Roger said once Nick was out of earshot.

"You were cheating on me."

His face flushed dull red, enough of a confirmation to give her a slight pang, a little sting of betrayal. Maybe she had cared for Roger after all. Her feelings for Roger and Nick were like water and wine. If you'd never had a really good merlot or pinot noir you wouldn't miss it. But once you'd taken that first sip, you couldn't go back to water.

"How did you know?" he finally said. "Lindy—"

"Had no clue. It took me a while to figure out why you were acting so strangely that last month we were together. And then you dumped me without any warning. The only thing that made sense was that you'd found someone else to run your errands."

"Missy didn't run my errands, and I dumped— You and I broke up because I got cold feet. But that was a mistake."

Right, mistake, Emmy thought. He'd probably come to that conclusion right after *Missy* dumped him. She couldn't bring herself to say it out loud, though. Satisfying as it would be, Roger was clearly upset and hurting, and if she added to that she'd only feel bad about it later. The last thing she wanted on her first day of vacation with Nick was to be thinking about Roger. With any luck he'd be history after tonight. Ancient history.

"Roger—"

"We belong together, Emily, but I didn't come here to beg. Lindy contacted me about the house." He took a minute, put on a pretty good show of hurt and indignation. "You didn't have to sic your lawyer on me. I wasn't serious about suing you. I just wanted to talk."

Emmy had to reach deep to find some patience. "There's really no point, Roger."

"Look, I know I hurt you." He reached out.

Emmy took a step back, and he got the idea, dropping his hand.

"If you could please just—"

"I thought you didn't come here to beg."

He took a step forward this time. His expression was pretty dark, but it was just Roger not getting his way. There was no real threat there.

"It's over," Emmy said. "You did us both a favor by calling off the wedding when you did. We weren't in love, we shouldn't have gotten married."

"You don't mean that."

"Yes, I do." She held out her hand, his engagement ring between her thumb and forefinger. "I think you should have this back."

Roger simply stared at it for what felt like an eternity, then he reached out and took the ring. He slipped it into his pocket, looked at Nick, standing behind Emmy in the open doorway, and shook his head.

"Maybe you weren't in love," he said, "but I was. You never really wanted that, at least not from me. You preferred…a certain amount of distance, and I didn't take the time out of my life to do anything about it. I thought once we were married—"

"Are you forgetting about Missy?" Nick chimed in.

Roger shot Nick a glare but addressed Emmy. "Like I said, Missy was a mistake, a spur-of-the-moment thing that got out of hand. When I met her… Well, I guess I didn't realize something was missing from our relationship until I stumbled across it."

Nick started for Roger.

Emmy stepped in front of him. "No, let him say what he has to say."

"So he can dump all the blame on you? Because that's what he's trying to do. You're rejecting him and he wants to make sure he hurts you back."

"I'm not trying to hurt you, Emily," Roger said. "I came here to tell you I'm still in love with you. I'm not foolish enough to think that's going to mean anything after what I did to you, but at least I'm saying it with my eyes wide open."

"What's that supposed to mean?" Emmy asked him.

Roger started to snap back at her, then thought better of it, shaking his head instead. "I said I didn't come here to hurt you, and that's the truth. But I wouldn't be doing you any favors if I didn't tell you to ask yourself how long this guy—" he jerked his head to Nick "—is going to hang around, waiting for you to stop being so afraid of hurt and rejection that you can't open up and let anyone into your heart."

Roger held her eyes a minute longer, and then he walked away.

Nick put his arms around her, resting his chin on her shoulder. They watched Roger get into his car across the street and drive away.

Emmy shut the door and moved away from Nick, but she didn't go back into the bedroom, either. Spending the next few days with Nick seemed wrong now. Oh, she knew Roger wanted to get to her, to hurt her, just like Nick said. That didn't mean he hadn't told the truth. She was closed off. She did expect to get hurt. She'd been hurt so many times that she'd stopped waiting for someone to come along who really loved her—which was probably never going to happen because she kept her distance from everyone so she didn't get hurt. A vicious circle.

Nick had been so patient, so persistent, but what if she couldn't open up to him? Would he get tired of waiting for her to get over the scars foster care had left on her heart? And should she get over her childhood at all? Wasn't that what had made her who she was? Sure, parts of it had left her wounded, too, but she wasn't a total loss as a human being, or a woman for that matter. Nick hadn't declared his feelings, but if he did love her, shouldn't he accept her the way she was, faults and all?

"What's going on in there?" he asked, tapping a finger against her temple.

"I—I really don't know." She was so mixed up, so worried and unsure again of what she wanted from Nick and what he would be willing to accept from her.

And then there was Roger.

"You did the right thing, Emmy," Nick said. "Returning his ring was exactly what you needed to do in order to get your point across."

"I hope so," Emmy said. Problem was, she didn't believe it. In his way, Roger was every bit as persistent as Nick was. Once he decided he wanted something, he generally found a way to get it. And if he didn't get it he got angry. And Roger was a small, vindictive man when he was angry.

EMMY TOOK the camisole and went back into her room. Nick followed her, but she was just standing there, staring at her suitcase, not finishing the packing.

Not good, Nick thought. She was withdrawing into herself again, right in front of his eyes. It made him mad—hell, it made him sorry he hadn't punched Roger in the face. After all the time it had taken him to bring her around to seeing the possibilities between them, a few well-aimed words from a man who knew her every vulnerability had brought them back to square one.

She was feeling guilty about sending Roger on his way, worried that taking a risk was only asking for heartache. Nick wasn't having it. When she sighed for the third time, he decided that not bringing the subject up wasn't helping her forget about it.

"You did what you had to do, Emmy," he said, and if his voice was a bit rough, a little impatient, maybe she needed to think about how he was feeling. "Don't let him get to you."

"I'm not. It's just…Maybe it would be better if you went home, Nick. I'm not really in the mood for company."

That hit him like a slap to the face, being called company after what they'd been to each other. Maybe it had only been one night, but she knew he wanted more from her. Which was exactly the problem, thanks to Roger.

It might have been selfish on Nick's part, but he wasn't giving her a choice. "You're stuck with me," he said. He snapped her suitcase shut, took her by the hand and towed her out of the bedroom.

They made it to the front door before he realized what he was doing. And what he could be destroying.

"Emmy?" He waited until she focused on him, and then until she actually saw him. "Let's just start with dinner, okay?"

She looked into Nick's earnest, uncertain face and didn't have the heart to disappoint him. He didn't deserve this, she thought to herself. And she didn't deserve him, a tiny version of Roger's voice said in her brain. That, more than anything, made up her mind for her. Roger had dumped her; he had no right coming back and making her worry, and doubt and feel bad about herself.

She retrieved her overnight bag, shut off the lights and followed Nick out of the house, locking up behind her. They didn't talk on the drive. Emmy tried not to think, as well. Her thoughts weren't very cheerful at the moment, or encouraging.

Just hours ago her course had been so clear. Now she had no idea what she was doing, or why. It was only worse when they got back to Nick's, and the place hit her exactly as it had the first time she'd been there. It wasn't just a house, but a home that was filled with love. And love was something she knew nothing about.

"So," Nick said, clearly feeling as uncomfortable as she was, "do you want to go out for dinner, or order in?"

"I'm kind of tired, Nick. I didn't really get any sleep last night, and now…"

Nick dropped her suitcase at the foot of the stairs and pulled her into his arms. "I'm sorry, Emmy, I shouldn't have brought you back here, knowing you weren't sure. But I couldn't stand to leave you there, alone and hurt. We don't have to talk if you don't want to, but I'm not going anywhere, and neither are you. Otherwise Roger wins."

He sounded so upset, so angry. Emmy wrapped her arms around him to comfort him and realized she was the one taking comfort from the embrace. And Nick was right. If she let Roger get to her, she was giving him exactly what he wanted. She'd be damned if she let him win. After everything, she'd be damned.

Roger had known her a lot longer than Nick, and apparently he'd known her a lot better than she'd ever suspected. And yet he'd never made an ounce of effort to help her open up. Instead, he'd used her fear against her, let her keep him at an emotional arm's length because it suited him. Until it didn't, and then he'd used it against her, trying to make her take a step backward, into the familiar. He didn't care if it was good for her, as long as it was good for him.

The worst of it all was, she'd taken it out on Nick. She hadn't yelled, or made accusations, or called him names. She'd done something a lot worse. She'd pulled away, and it would have served her right if he didn't want anything to do with her ever again. But, incredibly, he did. He was still there for her, as no one in her life had ever been. If she turned her back on him—

No, this would be turning her back on herself, on the things she'd learned and the progress she'd made. Nick might or might not be in her future, but there was no getting away from herself. It would be nice, for a change, not to feel damaged and hopeless, to face a Saturday and not feel desperate because she didn't have work to hide in. It would be nice to stop thinking of her future in terms of how long her current job would last and start thinking of it in terms of having an actual life with a husband, maybe even children.

The thought of it, of all that commitment, scared her half to death. But she wasn't giving birth tomorrow, she reminded herself. And every journey started with one single step.

Her first step wasn't a step at all. She closed her eyes and leaned into Nick, let him give her comfort and gave herself permission to take it. In all her life there'd never been anyone who understood what she felt, what she needed, and cared enough to give it. Nick did, and it touched her.

She leaned back, lifted her hand to his cheek, and tried out a smile. "I make a mean grilled cheese sandwich," she said, suddenly hungry, and for more than food.

Nick lifted her off her feet and hugged her tightly enough to force the breath from her. She held on just as tightly to him, and when he slipped an arm around her waist, she did the same, and they walked into the kitchen together.

They made dinner and ate in front of the TV. Nick put on a channel that consisted completely of reruns. *Lassie, Lost in Space, Dennis the Menace.*

"Chicken noodle soup, grilled cheese sandwiches and *Gilligan's Island* reruns," Emmy said. "I feel like I'm twelve years old." *For the first time,* she added silently, because she didn't want Nick feeling sorry for her again.

"Oh, man," he said, "I had plans for you, and you just ruined them."

"Plans?"

"It's okay, Emmy, we can just sit here and watch TV and hold hands."

"Maybe I had plans for you."

"Plans?" he repeated with just the same put-on innocence she'd used.

"I have a suitcase full of lingerie upstairs, and you have all these fantasies…"

"You think you can make me forget about Maryann and Ginger?"

Emmy punched him on the arm and tried to scramble up from the couch.

Nick snagged her around the waist and hauled her down on top of him. "You're the only woman I've thought of that way since we met." He brushed her hair out of her face. "Emmy, I—"

She put her fingers over his lips, then replaced them with her mouth. She didn't want words, especially the kind that came along with expectations. Not that Nick would say something in order to get her to declare her feelings, but there were some words that carried so much weight they demanded a response. Even if it was silence.

Emmy preferred to let her actions speak for her, and what her actions were saying was, "now." She ran her hands under his shirt, braced herself and dove into him. No holding back, and she used every weapon in her limited sexual arsenal, some she didn't even know she possessed. She just did what came naturally, using her mouth, her hands, her body, to satisfy her hunger to be held, to be cherished, to be needed. If she could, she'd have burrowed inside Nick's skin, her yearning to be with him was that extreme.

Nick took her upper arms in his hands and gently pushed her away. His eyes met hers, held for one humming moment, and then he dragged her back against him, fumbling with her clothes even as she fought with his. And when they came together again, bare skin against bare skin, the air around them seemed to ignite.

Nick took his mouth to her breast, shot her up so fast her head spun and every nerve ending in her body was on fire. Emmy refused to go over without him. Since she happened to be on top at the moment, she straddled him. She watched his eyes go dark and hot when she took him in, watched the fierceness that came over his face when she started to move. And when he caught her hips in his hands and began to move with her, she went blind with desperation, breathless with need. Mindless.

Friction built, layered sensation over sensation, heat tore through her, burned away everything but the scent, the feel, the power and vulnerability of the man she was taking. The man who was taking her. Everything she wanted, everything he gave crashed together inside her, a tightly controlled explosion that tore a sob out of her, swamped her on wave after wave of something far too intense to be called mere pleasure.

"Jeez, Emmy," Nick groaned, "I think you killed me."

She opened one eye, faintly surprised there wasn't smoke coming out of her ears, then propped herself up on shaky arms, grinning at the sight of him.

He was still wearing his shirt and socks, his pants and boxers knotted around one ankle. "You look alive to me," she said. "Used, but alive."

He grinned over that, plucking her bra off her shoulder and tossing it aside. "You look pretty used yourself."

"I don't think I have the energy left to make it upstairs, that's for sure."

"Heck," Nick said, "I don't think I can make it back to the couch."

Emmy looked around. "How'd we get on the floor?"

"Gravity. And exuberance." Nick levered himself to his feet and pulled her up with him, then tripped on his pants and fell on the couch.

Since he'd dragged her down with him, Emmy decided it was fate. Nick reached up and turned off the lamp, Emmy pulled the throw from the back of the couch over them, snuggled back against him, and dropped like a stone into sleep.

Chapter Fifteen

Nick's refrigerator contained the staples of single men everywhere: eggs, cheese, beer, milk for his coffee and something slimy in one of the drawers. Emmy closed the refrigerator and checked the cupboards. Oyster crackers, probably stale, canned soup, an empty Twinkies box with an inch of dust on it. Clearly, Nick didn't count grocery shopping among his regular activities.

"I've been meaning to get to the market."

She whipped around, hand to heart, and there he was, standing in the kitchen doorway, rumpled and sleepy-eyed. Her pulse spiked for an entirely different reason. She decided it was the sexy, suggestive way he was looking at her. And, as usual, she realized that eye contact wasn't in her best interest.

She had an agenda, and it started with food.

"It looks like the grilled cheese and soup last night just about cleaned you out," she said, "but I can make French toast." She went back to the fridge, and retrieved the milk and eggs.

"Or we could go out for breakfast."

"You mean lunch? It's almost noon."

"If we go back upstairs, we don't have to worry about what meal it is."

His voice slid over her, warm, tempting, sneaking around

her defenses to tiptoe along her nerve endings and turn them against her. Nick came over, wrapped his arms around her waist and pressed himself against her. He smelled great, too, warm and male. Her knees went to water, her head spun, and she bobbled the eggs.

"Whatever meal it is, you almost lost it," Emmy managed in a voice that was reminiscent of Marilyn Monroe singing "Happy Birthday, Mr. President." She took a couple of deep breaths, put a few feet between her and Nick, and kept her eyes off him. Of course, it was hard to prevent him from making physical contact if she didn't see him coming. There were parts of her that wondered why physical contact was such a bad idea, but she chose to ignore those parts.

Thankfully, Nick sat at the table, which she could tell from the creaking of his chair. Normally it would have bothered her that he didn't feel any inclination to lend a hand, but since it was a pretty good bet that his hand would have landed somewhere on her person, and her person would turn traitor on her, she decided to be grateful for that, too. But not too grateful. "You're doing the dishes," she said to him.

"Darn, I thought I'd make a grocery list after we ate."

Now Emmy looked at him, and she managed not to lose her head. Nobody made fun of her lists. "I think you'd better leave that to the expert."

He smiled at her, just like the first time he'd smiled at her, and she couldn't give a hang about the list. That was really bad, since she'd determined to make the next four days about more than sex.

She cracked eggs into a bowl, wondering if she was crazy for thinking they could last for even four days, let alone four weeks or months. Or years. They had such different temperaments…which was the same as saying ice was cold, she thought with a smile. She and Nick were polar opposites, night and day, Lucy and Ricky.

She was self-motivated, he wasn't motivated at all… She got a flashback from the previous night, but she stuck with her original assessment. Sex, she decided, didn't count. He was easygoing, she was strung like a kite at full sail. He floated through life like a helium balloon, she was more of a steam roller, regulated by an atomic clock.

It would be insane to get any more involved with Nick Porter.

She still had issues from her childhood. So did he, and the worst part was he didn't want to face his issues, let alone work through them. But she wanted to face hers. Thanks to him.

Oh, Roger and Jerry had helped, too, but mostly it was thanks to Nick that she was caught between wanting to belong somewhere and abject terror that she'd get what she wanted. And the worst part of it was, they hadn't had one real, meaningful conversation in the entire time they'd known each other—and that counted work, since Nick managed to sidestep every discussion that involved actual decision-making. What kind of foundation was that to build a relationship on?

"So," she said, going to the French doors to pull the drapes open and let in the morning sun. She shrieked, hand to heart again because there was a dog staring in at her.

"It's Tripod," Nick said, "he's harmless."

Harmless, maybe, but he was also kind of freaky. And it had nothing to do with a missing leg. "What does he want?"

Nick shrugged. "A handout probably. Or maybe some attention."

Nick flipped open the paper she'd retrieved earlier, ignoring the dog. Emmy tried to do the same, but it was difficult since Tripod wouldn't go away. Kind of like Nick. Stubborn, persistent, and when the man decided he wanted something, the depth of his determination was staggering. And a little scary.

Emmy sighed, pouring milk into the bowl and whipping it together with the eggs. Even if she'd wanted to, it was too late to shut Nick out. She'd cracked the door to her private life far enough to let him slip in, but she was going to have to open it wider because his life was full of people—and three-legged dogs.

"So," she started again, "we always talk about work. Tell me about yourself."

"Not much to tell, really." Nick got up and opened a doorway Emmy had missed. It led into a small pantry. He pulled a bottle of maple syrup out, collected the butter from the refrigerator and sat back down. "And anyway, I'd rather talk about you. Tell me everything."

"Everything?"

He grinned. "In chronological order."

"You already know everything. My parents died when I was four, I lived in foster homes after that. Graduated from Boston College, degrees in Business and Process Engineering. I worked for a large engineering firm for a couple of years, then started Jones Consulting, and here I am."

Nick took the butter and syrup to the table and came back to pour himself a cup of coffee, appropriating the milk. He leaned back against the counter and took a sip. "Do you always work twice as hard as everyone else?"

When you came from where she did, Emmy thought, there were two roads to take: hard work or the easy path that led to nowhere. "There's nothing wrong with hard work," was all she said.

"No, but it would probably be easier if you worked for someone else. You wouldn't have to worry about where your next paycheck was coming from."

That was true, too. Instead she'd have worked eighty hours a week, fighting her way up a career path that was still predominately male. She'd have made half the money along the way, which meant she'd still be paying off her student loans. And worst of all, she'd have been surrounded by people who pretended to be her friends while they stepped on her in order to get the next promotion.

"It must've been hard going into business for yourself," Nick prompted.

· Emmy shrugged, slid French toast onto plates and carried them to the table. "It took a little while to get off the ground," she said as she set a plate in front of him and took her seat, "but when you start with nothing, it's not such a scary place to be."

There was no talking for a minute, silverware clinking on plates, butter being passed, the syrup bottle burping.

"What about you?" she asked him.

"I went to college," he said.

"For?"

"Liberal Arts. I liked everything, so I could never quite narrow it down to one subject."

Typical Nick, Emmy thought indulgently. "Did you want to take over Porter and Son?"

"I must have. There any more French toast?" he asked before Emmy could come up with another question.

She slid her plate over to him, settling for coffee now that her appetite was completely gone.

"You said you lived in a foster home," Nick said. "Did you like it?"

"Homes," she corrected him, "and no."

He looked up from the already empty plate. "One of them must have been okay?"

"Nothing like this," Emmy said, looking around the kitchen, its fixtures comfortably broken in from years of use. The table was nicked, the chairs creaked and the drapes were so old they ought to be collecting Social Security. And she knew that every scar on every stick of furniture must hold a memory. Not all of them were necessarily good, but they were all Nick's.

She wondered what it must be like for him to come into this room every morning, to remember the times his mother had made him breakfast and sent him off to school or outside to play. Emmy would have loved to hear him tell her how that felt, but she couldn't ask about his mom, it just hurt too much. And she couldn't ask him about his father now that she knew how painful an issue that was.

She was searching for a safe subject when Nick stood up, took her hand and pulled her to her feet. She went into his arms with almost no urging, sank into a kiss that tasted like maple syrup and felt like coming home—not to mention it was the safest subject there was between her and Nick. The one where they didn't do any talking at all.

THE REST of the week passed in a haze. A lot of sex, no real intimacy. Not that Emmy didn't make an effort on her own. She and Nick might not be able to talk about important personal issues just yet, but it didn't mean she intended to throw away a perfectly good opportunity to learn some things about herself, now that she'd recognized the need and found the willpower. It was a constant battle, fighting her own nature to see if she could fit herself into Nick's lifestyle. It nearly killed her, but she didn't look at her day planner once, she shut off her cell phone, and left her wristwatch in her purse… Okay, she wore her wristwatch, but it was on the wrong wrist, which made her cognizant of how many times a day she looked at it.

She slept till noon, she didn't eat regular meals, and the only exercise she got was in bed. By Sunday morning she figured she'd as good as run a marathon. She also figured she was going to blow a gasket if she didn't get five minutes of alone time. She liked being with Nick, but she liked being by herself, too.

She'd gotten up early and gone down to the kitchen. Nick was right upstairs, close enough that she didn't feel alone, far enough that she was alone. It was too early for the neighborhood to be jumping with activity. No dogs being walked, no lawns being mowed, skateboards, bicycles and scooters safely locked away in backyard sheds.

She took her coffee out to the patio, savoring the stillness, the absolute lack of activity outside—if she didn't count the three-legged dog sitting patiently beside her chair, staring at her. Tripod seemed to have an insatiable crush on Nick, but at least, Emmy thought, she'd learned to ignore his presence.

The sun was rising in a cloudless blue sky, chirping birds were the only sounds, and all she smelled was fresh morning air. Knowing it would change in a short while made her appreciate it so much more. So much, in fact, that she felt absolutely no need to be busy. Working meant she'd miss this precious hour of peace and quiet, so for once in her life she gave herself permission to be idle. It felt pretty good, too.

Tomorrow they went back to work, she and Nick. There would be other stresses layered over the personal ones between them, but for this hour, she was letting everything go.

"I wish I had a camera," Nick said from behind her.

Emmy was so relaxed her heart didn't even bump. "It is a pretty morning, isn't it?"

"I was talking about you and the dog."

She glanced down, realized that somewhere along the line she'd begun to rub Tripod's ears.

"You look right at home."

She felt right at home, too, which was something of an amazement to her.

Nick came the rest of the way out and took the chair next to hers. "You snuck out of bed again," he said.

"You were snoring like a lumberjack."

"You've slept with a lumberjack?"

She shrugged. "The point is, there was no sneaking."

"It looks like there's relaxing, though."

"There's definitely relaxing." Emmy looked over at him and smiled. "It's so quiet, which your neighborhood usually isn't, that I just had to sit here and enjoy it for a little while."

"I thought maybe you were getting restless, you know, five days cooped up here with me."

"Nope, not feeling cooped up. Maybe a bit restless." She smiled to take the sting out of her words. "It's been a long while since I took this much time off all at once, and never with a man."

"Not even Roger?"

She shook her head. "No, but we would have been on our honeymoon now."

Nick didn't say anything, and when she glanced over he was looking off into the distance.

"I'm sorry, I shouldn't have said that."

"I brought him up," Nick pointed out, turning to meet her eyes, "and you can talk about anything you want to, as long as you tell me you're not regretting anything on that score."

"I am, but they're regrets over my actions, my decision to settle for Roger when I didn't really love him."

"And what about us?"

Emmy leaned forward in her chair, and when he wouldn't face her, she reached over and took his hand. "Do you think I'm settling for you, Nick?"

"Not really, it's just… I'm not sure what you're doing here."

"Well." She sat back, wondering at the little burst of panic inside her, the fear that if she didn't declare her feelings for

Nick, he'd walk away. Problem was, she didn't know exactly what her feelings were. Or maybe she wasn't quite ready to admit them to herself.

"It's been less than a week—and I realize you think that's an excuse," she said when his body language screamed as much. "But it's the truth, too, Nick. We've only known each other three weeks. I've loved every second of the time we've spent together, but we haven't talked about anything important, heck, we haven't gotten out of bed for the last five days except to eat. I've barely had time to think, let alone sort out my emotions."

He let out his breath, seeming to relax a little, although he still didn't look at her. "I kind of pushed you into this, didn't I?"

"I haven't done anything I didn't want to do."

Now he turned, and this time he took her hand. "After what you've been through in the last little while, I guess I can understand you being a little gun-shy, Emmy. Only… This is new to me, too."

"Then we'll figure it out together." She squeezed his hand. "Just not this second, okay?"

"How about after lunch," Nick said.

Mostly he was teasing, but there was a little bit of serious in his tone, too, and it hurt Emmy to know she was causing him any upset. But he hadn't said he loved her, either. "How about after you answer the phone," she said when she heard it ringing.

Nick didn't look too happy about the interruption, but he headed into the kitchen. The ringing stopped, Emmy heard Nick's deep voice, the words unintelligible, and a few seconds later he reappeared with the phone in his hand.

Emmy took it, her puzzled frown turning into an ear-to-ear grin when she heard the voice on the other end. "How did you know I was here?" she said to Lindy.

"I've been trying to call you all week. You're not answering your cell phone, and you're not listening to the messages on your answering machine, because I've left a half dozen and you haven't called me back. So either I did something to tick you off—not likely since you never stay mad at me for long—or you had a really good reason for not returning my calls."

"Maybe I've been busy."

"Getting busy, more like."

Emmy felt her cheeks heat, but she laughed because it was a good heat, and Lindy meant her comment in a good way.

"So tell me," she said, "how is Nick?"

"He's fine." Emmy cut her eyes to the man in question, but he'd disappeared into the kitchen.

"I wasn't talking about his health."

"I know. I haven't felt this relaxed in years." Maybe never, Emmy added to herself. "And that's the only detail you're getting out of me."

"So you're happy then?"

"Yes."

"Just yes? No buts? Because I know you, Emmy. Whenever anything good happens you don't let yourself enjoy it because you're too busy bracing yourself for when the bad comes along."

"Ouch." That was true, but that had been her experience in life. Happiness was a rainbow that lasted for seconds. The storm clouds always came back, and they seemed to hang overhead forever. "You're right, Lindy, but for once I'm not borrowing trouble. Bad stuff has happened, and I don't seem to be dwelling on it."

Even more amazing, it was absolutely true. All the drama that had gone on before the last five days seemed to have melted out of her mind. When Lindy asked the inevitable question, she had to wrack her brain to recount her meetings with Mrs. Runion and Jerry. In fact, those moments seemed so long ago, the upheaval that had come along with them was nothing more than an annoyance now.

"Oh," she added almost as an afterthought, "I gave Roger his ring back, and I think he's finally gone for good."

"Hallelujah. I'm ripping up the power of attorney even as we speak."

Emmy laughed. "Thanks for running interference for me, Lindy."

"You're welcome. And we're still on for dinner, right?"

"Shoot," Emmy said, "I forgot."

"You forgot?" Lindy said, shocked. "When's the last time you looked at your day planner?"

"Um… Wednesday, I think."

"Well, well. I never thought I'd see the day you forgot work, your best friend, everything, over a man. You do have it bad, don't you?"

Any answer Emmy gave was bound to get her in trouble. Nick was inside, but the windows were open, and she wouldn't put eavesdropping past him. That's what she'd be doing in his place.

The last five days had been great, but she needed some distance from him, a little while to herself to process where they'd been and where they were going. And where she wanted to go with Nick. If he heard her say that, though, he wouldn't understand. He'd think she didn't have any feelings for him, and she did. She just needed to figure out what they were before she got in over her head.

And she couldn't think of anyone better able to help her sort herself out than her best friend. "We're still on for dinner," she said to Lindy.

"Then put on something amazing and we'll make the men of this town swallow their tongues."

"Okay," she laughed. "Pick me up at my house at seven." And she disconnected, just in time for Nick to rejoin her on the patio.

He didn't look happy.

Chapter Sixteen

"You're going out to dinner with Lindy," Nick said, not bothering to hide the fact that he had been listening to her conversation. "I'll go with you."

"You'd give up the big baseball game tonight to have dinner with two women?" Emmy asked him.

"I'm giving up the game to be with you," he said, although in all honesty he'd forgotten about the game. "I want to be with you. In case Roger shows up." Or anyone else Nick didn't want her running into, namely any member of her foster families. At least not without him around to make sure those meetings weren't horrible for her.

"That's sweet, Nick, but I gave Roger his ring back. I don't think he's going to be a problem anymore. You know what is a problem, though? I don't have a car."

Perfect, Nick thought, his shoulders sagging in relief. "I'll drive you."

Emmy got up and came over to him, and when he thought it best to avoid her gaze, she framed his face in her hands and waited for him to meet his eyes.

"What's going on?" she asked him. "Why are you being so protective—overprotective?"

"I'm not being overprotective..." He tried to hold out, but

it was no use. "Okay," he finally relented, "you've been having such a hard time lately, I just wanted to stick close for a little while, keep creeps like Jerry away from you."

Creeps like himself, Nick thought sourly, since he was the reason Jerry had imposed himself on her. But maybe she'd made progress. Between Mrs. Runion and Jerry and what Roger had said to her— Okay, not Roger. After Roger had gotten through with her she'd been upset, withdrawn. She hadn't wanted to spend the rest of the week with Nick, but she'd come over anyway. Because he'd given her the room to make the decision for herself, no pressure, no judgment, and she was strong enough to see that closing herself off only doomed her to a long, lonely life. Seen in that light, Nick decided, he'd actually helped her start down the road to letting go of the past and opening herself to love.

Didn't that mean he could call off the other two foster families he'd managed to contact? Or was that just a self-serving justification to keep her from finding out what he'd started and hating him for it? It definitely felt selfish, and he was trying to reason his way through this thing so that whatever decision he made was in Emmy's best interest—

"I'm a big girl, Nick," she said. "I've been handling creeps by myself for a long time."

—and it was time for him to take a step back. He slipped an arm around her waist and snugged her against his side. "At least tell me where you're going."

"Don't know," she said, "but Lindy told me to wear something sexy so we can pick up guys." She smiled up at him. "Don't worry, I'll only bring home a couple."

Nick curved his lips, but he wasn't really feeling it. "I guess I have been overprotective."

She snorted softly. "Just slightly. Really, Nick, you have to trust me. If you don't, this isn't going to work."

"I do trust you. And this is going to work."

"Okay, then I'll see you tomorrow." She stretched up on her toes to give him a peck on the lips.

Nick gathered her close, close enough to know a kiss, even one as deep and mind-stealing as this one, wasn't enough. For either of them.

"You sure you don't want me to come over later?" he whispered, his lips still against hers.

"Tomorrow," Emmy said.

He sighed, ran his hands down her arms to link his fingers with hers, but he didn't push. "I'm used to sleeping with you in my arms," he said. "I'll miss you."

"I'll miss you, too," Emmy said. "More than you know." She put as much reassurance into her words, her eyes, as she could, but she didn't get the blinding smile she'd expected. It really worried her. "A night apart isn't the end of the world," she said gently, "and I'll see you first thing in the morning, at Porter and Son."

Nick didn't say anything, just wrapped his arms around her and held her close for the longest time. Emmy closed her eyes and simply enjoyed it, until a thought intruded on the peaceful moment.

"Just one more thing," she said. "Can you give me a ride home?"

"I'D SAY you handled that pretty well," Lindy said.

"Yeah, I'm proud of myself." Emmy leaned forward and traded the carton of fried rice for the cashew chicken. While she was at it, she exchanged the chopsticks in her hand for a fork. "I've never really mastered these things," she said.

"Shhh, the dumb blonde is about to go into the basement, despite the creepy music and the fact that four of her friends have gone down there and not returned."

Emmy took that as her cue to shut her eyes and plug her ears. Instead of going to a restaurant, they'd opted to order takeout and rent movies. Since Emmy had gotten to pick the food, the movies had been Lindy's choice. Emmy had made this obviously flawed decision despite the fact that Lindy always chose horror movies—the gorier the better—because in the four days she'd been at Nick's, there'd been a lot of quick thrown-together meals, but not a vegetable in sight, and she could all but feel her arteries hardening.

After a few minutes, Lindy nudged her and she cautiously unplugged her ears. When she didn't hear any screaming—or crunching or squishy murder sounds—she opened her eyes.

"I stopped playing that joke on you as soon as you got it," Lindy said. "The fourth time I pulled it."

"You mean when I gave up on the hope you'd act like an adult?"

Lindy stuck out her tongue.

Emmy rolled her eyes—and got up to answer the door when the bell rang.

"Fifty bucks says it's Nick," Lindy called after her.

Emmy ignored her, which wasn't much of a strain since the sight of the man standing on her doorstep left her speechless. She stood there, she didn't know how long, staring at him. Then she stepped back and swung the door shut.

The doorbell rang again.

Lindy came out of the living room, took one look at Emmy's face, and said, "It's not Nick."

Emmy shook her head.

Lindy squinted through the peep and said, "He doesn't look like a crazed killer or anything."

"You'd know," Emmy muttered. But instead of a snappy comeback or a goofy face, Lindy pulled the door open. Unfortunately the man was still standing there, and of course Lindy asked the obvious question.

"Joe Esterhaus," was the answer she got.

Lindy shut the door in his face, turned to Emmy. "Do you know a Joe Esterhaus?"

Emmy pulled in a careful breath, then let it out just as deliberately. "I used to," she said when she felt steadier. "He was a foster brother. The last house I lived in before I turned eighteen."

Lindy mulled that over for a minute, then opened the door. "Go away," she said.

"But—"

"Now, or I call the cops."

Emmy stepped over to the window and peeked through the drapes. Joe stuffed his hands in his pockets, mouth tight, looking pretty miserable before he turned and strode off down the sidewalk.

Lindy closed the door again and shot the deadbolt home just in case. "He was kind of cute," she said, as if she hadn't just slammed the door in his face twice and threatened him with a trip to the pokey.

Emmy went back into the living room and dropped down onto the couch, drawing her legs up, wrapping her arms around them and resting her cheek on her knees.

Lindy followed her in. She didn't say anything, letting her have her moment—and that's about all it was. Lindy wasn't known for her patience. "So give already," she said. "What's going on in there?"

Emmy tried a one-shoulder shrug that didn't quite work in her current position. She lifted her head and said, "I'm starting to realize some things."

"Because of Joe Esterhaus?"

"No, it isn't the foster people. It's being with Nick."

"Are you going to explain that, or should I go scare up a psychic?"

Emmy gave her a weak smile. "Being with Nick… His childhood and mine were so different, almost exactly opposite, as a matter of fact."

"Let me guess," Lindy said, "he has issues too? No one gets to adulthood without baggage of some sort, Emmy."

Emmy took to her feet; moving them always seemed to help her put her thoughts in order. "Nick's life is so full," she began. "He's got all these friends at work, like an extended family, really, and he knows all his neighbors."

"Don't forget Stella."

"As if I could," Emmy said, but without the heat she might have used a week ago. "He had parents, Lindy, his own parents. A mom and a dad, but it wasn't all Norman Rockwell."

"I had a mom and dad of my own, too, remember? And Norman Rockwell would have run screaming from my house."

"I know, and I should have figured it out before this, but you're…"

"Damaged," Lindy said without rancor. "And Nick comes off like he's completely normal."

"Exactly, but he has issues, just like me, and I don't know, seeing that, it made me realize how closed off I am. How I settled for someone like Roger."

"Because you didn't think you deserved someone like Nick."

"More like I didn't deserve to be happy. And that was just…stupid."

"Well, all I can say is hooray for Nick. I hope you two will be very happy together."

Emmy sighed. "Me, too, but there's still the contract to get through."

"It's awfully windy in here all of a sudden."

"I'm going to have to say some hard things to him," Emmy said, stifling another sigh, "so I guess my future happiness depends on how well he takes it."

"Emmy…" Lindy struggled for a second, then huffed out a breath. "I'm a big, fat coward."

"You're the furthest thing from a coward I know."

"Honey, it's all an act."

"Well, whatever it is, spit it out. Trust me, you'll feel better."

Lindy shook her head. "It's only… If things don't work out with Nick, don't let it send you back to square one. No matter what he does or says."

Emmy frowned. "Nick would never do anything to hurt me."

"Neither would I."

That was even more bewildering to Emmy. She started to ask what Lindy was talking about, but her best friend jumped up and disappeared into the kitchen. She came back a couple of minutes later with a tub of ice cream and two spoons. "I almost forgot," she said, "I picked up dessert along with the movies. And to hell with my diet."

Emmy grabbed a spoon, but she laid it on the coffee table.

"Okay," Lindy said, "but you don't know what you're missing." She dropped down on the sofa, took a big spoonful of ice cream, and talked around it. "It's coffee ice cream with chocolate chips and chocolate fudge, your two favorite flavors in the whole world."

Emmy collapsed on the sofa, too, memories of chocolate-covered coffee beans making her stomach roll. "Not anymore."

Chapter Seventeen

Nick slipped his arms around Emmy's waist, nuzzled the back of her neck. For a second she melted against him, then that annoying work ethic of hers kicked in.

"I thought you went out to get the suggestion box," she said, easing away and turning to face him.

"I did." He put it on his desk, which was now behind her, using the movement as an excuse to put his arms around her again. "Then I came back in here and you were leaning over the desk and the nape of your neck was right there... I couldn't help myself."

A smile tugged at Emmy's lips, but she held it off. She didn't push him away, though. "Work," she reminded him, tapping the box beside her.

She was weakening, Nick could see it. If not for that damned business/personal line she'd drawn, there'd be more than paperwork happening on his desk. "I missed you last night," he said, taking a moment to refamiliarize himself with the spot, right behind her ear, that always made her sigh.

She didn't disappoint him, but she didn't exactly melt into a compliant puddle, either.

"I missed you too, Nick, and we'll make up for it later. Tonight. I'll cook you dinner..." She stopped talking, probably because Nick was shaking his head. "I know there's been a lot of sandwiches and things out of cans, but I could cook you dinner…with instructions."

"There's no doubt in my mind," Nick said, "but this isn't about your skill in the kitchen. I have a thing tonight."

"A thing?"

"One of my father's oldest friends," Nick said absently, because he was wracking his brain for a way to get out of it—and not finding one. "Every year he throws this big party."

"Then you have to go," Emmy said.

"And you have to come with me."

That did it. All the progress he'd made with Emmy flew out the window, chased away by the instantaneous panic his invitation seemed to have caused.

"We don't have to stay very long."

"No, Nick, I—I appreciate the offer, but I'm just not ready for old family friends yet."

He clamped down, hard, over the combination of annoyance and frustration and the urge to ask her when she would be ready. For the first time in his life he was in a hurry over something. Someone. He wanted Emmy to come around now, to stop living in the past and see what was right in front of her. But that was his timetable, and he wasn't so bound up in it that he couldn't see her side of the issue.

"Then I'll see you after?" he said, making it a question so she wouldn't feel boxed in.

She rewarded him by winding her arms around his neck and pulling him close. "Thank you for understanding," she said, her lips against his neck nearly destroying his newfound resolve.

Nick pulled back. He didn't know where he found the strength, but he did it, and just for good measure—and before he could change his mind—he put the desk between them.

"Suggestion box," he said, reaching into his desk drawer to retrieve the key.

"This thing looks even worse than it did last week," Emmy observed.

It was still charred, and now it looked as though somebody had taken a pry bar to it and when that didn't work, beaten the tar out of it. "It's all dented." Nick unlocked it but when Emmy tried to reach inside he blocked her. "You might want to wait until I make sure there's only paper in there. Remember the dead mouse," he reminded her.

She snatched her hand back, waiting until Nick gave her the all clear before she pulled out a stack of papers and started to read them, one by one, placing them into two piles.

Judging by the facial expressions that went along with each quick read, one pile was clearly for serious suggestions, the other wasn't. Since the two piles were relatively even, apparently Marty Henshaw wasn't the guy to convince all of the other employees that Emmy was there to help.

"So much for Marty's influence," Emmy said, clearly on the same wavelength.

"It would take an act of Congress to convince everyone."

Emmy was looking pretty grim, which kind of took the funny out of Nick's mood.

He freely acknowledged that he was about the most laid-back man in the world, but nobody should be as tightly strung as Emmy Jones. It wasn't natural. It wasn't fun. Emmy definitely needed to have some fun, and he was just the guy to provide it. Thankfully he had a convenient source of hilarity.

He reached for the suggestions, just as Emmy did. She took the serious ones, of course. Nick took the others. He started to read through them, laughing. He held up one, containing a diagram that could have come out of a sex manual. "I think we tried this," he said, handing Emmy the slip of paper.

Emmy's cheeks heated, but she was smiling again. "We didn't just try that, it worked. Really well, as I recall."

Nick tossed the paper over his shoulder and took her hand, pulling her around the desk and into his lap. The kiss started off slow and sweet, but it heated, involving tongues and nipping teeth and moaning. On both their parts. When hands began to get into the act, Emmy found the wits to scramble to her feet. Nick, a beat behind, let her go. The fact that she stood, hands flat on his desk, breathing hard, for a full minute while she gathered control, was pretty gratifying. Especially since he was doing some control-gathering of his own.

"Let's hope there's something useful in here," Emmy finally said. She picked up the serious stack, read and put aside the top two, then said, "here's something."

Nick took it from her, looked it over, and shook his head. "I still like my pile better." He read the next one and handed it to her, grinning.

"Get serious," Emmy said, tossing it aside.

"They're laughing with you, Emmy, not at you. Lighten up."

"I could, but while you're laughing with them, things around here are only getting worse."

Nick bit down on what he wanted to say, taking the stack of suggestions out of Emmy's hand.

"There are some decent ideas in there," she said. "They only require an open mind to see the possibilities."

Nick went through them, but in light of her comment, stubbornness had already predisposed him to his answer. "I don't see anything workable."

"Because you don't want them to be."

"That doesn't make any sense."

"No, it doesn't, since change is the only thing that stands between you and bankruptcy. But I guess your employees will find other jobs when Porter and Son goes belly-up."

Nick tossed the slips of paper down on the desk. "We're not going belly-up."

"Yes you are, and it's time for you to face it. I've looked at your books, Nick. Two years ago you were making a small profit. A year later you were breaking even, now you're losing money. Sales are on a steady decline—"

"I have enough to pay you, don't worry." He knew he'd crossed the line, saw the hurt flash over her face before she shut down again, and cursed himself. But dammit she was like a broken record. *You have to change, Nick, the company will go under if you don't do things differently.* He was tired of hearing it, tired of fighting to get Emmy to do things his way during working hours—and the rest of the time as well. "I'm sorry," he said, "I guess this whole thing is starting to get to me."

"Something is," Emmy said with a little snap to her voice. "Something was bothering you all last week—"

"I'm worried, that's all."

"And I'm trying to help you find a solution so you won't have to worry anymore."

Nick nodded. Of course she assumed he was talking about Porter and Son when it was really Emmy weighing on his mind. He thought he'd hidden his guilt and concern pretty well last week, but she'd seen right through him. Any other woman would have asked, but only the fact that Emmy wasn't comfortable poking into his private feelings had stopped her from pushing him for an explanation. It had taken a lot of agonizing and an entire week, but Nick had finally seen the error of his ways. Better late than never, which would only be true if he managed to close the Pandora's box he'd opened once and for all, rather than following Emmy around and guarding her against the evils he'd unleashed on her. So he'd called off all her foster relatives, except for one guy by the name of Joe Esterhaus, and only because he couldn't get hold of him. But he would, soon.

Joe Esterhaus notwithstanding, Nick was so relieved to have the whole, misguided episode nearly over with that he didn't want to talk about anything depressing. And Porter and Son's predicament was depressing.

IF SOMEONE had asked her, Emmy would have said things couldn't get any worse. Her first day back to work with Nick and they'd almost broken up. Okay, maybe that was over-dramatizing events just slightly. But they'd certainly come close to having a full-blown argument, thanks to Nick's stubbornness. She'd barely touched on the subject of making changes at Porter and Son and he'd gone all... wonky, uptight, which, if she was being honest with herself, bothered her more than anything else. Nick wasn't an uptight kind of guy and knowing that she'd made him that way, well, the guilt was almost unbearable. Leaving Porter and Son, knowing it was on a path to oblivion, wasn't an option either.

After everything she'd been through in her life, she couldn't think of a time that had been more emotionally charged. Finding Roger waiting on her doorstep was just the capper to the day.

"What's next?" she asked him. "Am I going to come home one day to find you've pitched a tent on my front lawn?"

"There's no need to be insulting," Roger huffed.

"I've had a nasty day, Roger. I'm absolutely not in the mood to listen to whatever it is you have to say."

Roger opened his mouth anyway.

She cut him off. "I have two words for you. Restraining order."

"Not necessary," he bit off. "I get it, we're over."

"And yet you're not leaving."

"You've changed, Emily. You're more... You're just more. And you don't love me now. If you ever did."

She knew he was playing her emotions, knew he was

trying to get to her, but she still felt guilty. Not guilty enough to let him in her house. Keeping him out meant another confrontation on her front walk, but that was one of the benefits of not knowing her neighbors; if they noticed what had been going on at her house at least they couldn't ask her about it.

"What do you want, Roger?" she asked him, wearier than she could ever remember. "Tell me what it is so I can say no."

"And then I'll go away?" He shoved his hands in his pockets, his mouth twisting in a half smile. "We would be on our honeymoon right now, if I hadn't been an idiot."

"Roger…"

"Joe Esterhaus," he blurted out.

Emmy froze, just her eyes shifting to his.

"Pete Hannigan."

"How do you know about them?"

"The question you should be asking is how Nick Porter knows about them."

"I'm going inside now."

"Emily," he caught her wrist before she could put the key in her front-door lock. "You always preferred the plain truth."

She had, but suddenly she found the idea of wearing blinders very appealing. And that would only postpone the inevitable. "How do I know you're going to tell me the truth, and not something you've concocted to make Nick look bad?"

Roger shrugged. "I'll tell you what I know, you can ask him if it's true or not, and then make up your own mind."

She ought to tell him to leave, Emmy thought frantically. She knew it was a mistake to listen to Roger and then go to Nick. He'd be on the defensive, if he wasn't completely hurt and insulted that she'd even doubted him. And yet…And yet she couldn't let it go.

"Last Wednesday night," Roger began, taking her silence for agreement, "when I came here…"

Emmy made hurrying motions with her hands. "Get to the point."

"When Porter answered the door, he asked me if I was Joe Esterhaus or Pete Hannigan."

"Are those the only names he mentioned?"

"Why—" Roger slipped his hands in his pockets and rocked back on his heels. "Those aren't the only foster family members you've run across."

He managed to keep from smiling, but he couldn't keep the smugness from showing in his eyes. Emmy hated him in that moment, with a depth that shocked her. "When we got engaged I told you I was in foster care as a child, and you couldn't have cared less. Why are you so interested now?"

"Maybe you should be asking Nick Porter that question."

Emmy didn't speak. She could barely think around the sick suspicion growing inside her.

Roger wasn't content with spreading innuendo. "I had to call every Esterhaus and Hannigan in the phone book before I finally managed to locate the Esterhauses you lived with when you were in foster care. When I finally got hold of Joe, he told me someone named Nick Porter had called him and told him where to meet you."

Emmy backed up until she felt her front door behind her. Roger was still talking, but all she heard was a dull whooshing sound. The betrayal was so deep, the heartbreak so excruciating it was all she could do to keep from falling to pieces.

Roger took her hand in his. She yanked it free, rubbing the feel of his skin away.

"Look, Emily," he said, "I checked them out because I was curious. But how did he get their names? Foster records are sealed. You need a court order to look at…them…"

Emmy figured it out at the same time Roger did, and it made her even sicker to know that Lindy must have helped Nick.

"And what are you getting out of this, Roger? Did you think I would thank you? Did you expect me to be so grateful I'd take you back?"

"Well…" he sputtered out.

"I never want to see you again. Never."

"Fine," he snapped at her, "but I'm glad I ratted Porter out."

At least he'd picked an appropriate rodent, Emmy thought. She watched him walk away, opened her front door and locked it behind her, as automatically as if she'd been put on remote control. Certainly there was no feeling inside her, just a numb, gray fog that left her in a state of complete inertia.

She was still standing in the front entryway, still holding her briefcase, when Nick knocked on the door. She opened it, and feeling flooded in with the sight of him, pain such as she'd never imagined. She could feel her heart, not breaking but shriveling up into a hard, cold lump inside her chest. She'd loved him, then. She hadn't really been sure until just that second, when it had already become past tense.

She tried to tell herself Nick might still have an explanation for everything. But hope was a road she'd stepped off a long time ago. Because it was always a dead end.

"What's wrong?" he asked, walking past her.

She didn't quite trust her voice, so she took her time closing the door and going into the living room. When he sat beside her on the sofa she got up, unsteady legs and all, and moved to the armchair across from him. She couldn't bear to have him touch her. If he touched her she'd shatter into a million pieces that would never fit together again.

"Emmy?"

"Is it true?"

"Is what true?"

"Joe Esterhaus and Pete Hannigan. And Mrs. Runion and Jerry?"

He simply stared for a long, tense moment, then scrubbed a hand over his face. "It's true."

All the breath left her body in a rush, and the only thing that stopped her from putting her head between her knees was her absolute refusal to let him know how sick he'd made her.

"How did you know?" he asked quietly.

"Is that really what's important here?"

Nick shook his head and looked away. The muscles in his thighs tensed and for a minute Emmy thought he'd get up and simply walk away. No explanation, no apology, no regret for what he'd done.

But then he began to talk. His body language remained tense, his voice becoming more and more strained while Emmy felt herself going whiter and sicker. When he was done she did put her head between her knees, because as tempting as it was to throw up all over Nick, she'd have the shakes afterward, and she refused to let herself get debilitated before she'd said what needed to be said.

When she felt steady enough, she raised her head and made eye contact. This time it was Nick who looked away. "You sicced those people on me?"

"Not Mrs. Runion," he said. "She was an accident."

"But you dragged me to that fair, knowing…And you called Jerry."

"I wanted to help you get over the past, Emmy. I thought—"

"You thought?" She shot to her feet, the nausea gone, blasted away by a shockwave of fury and hurt. "Get out."

"Emmy."

She was halfway to the door when she turned back, stalked over and jammed a finger into his chest. "While you were *thinking,* did it occur to you that maybe you should tackle your own childhood issues before you stuck your nose into the middle of mine?"

"I'm not the one nursing emotional wounds from my childhood."

"Oh, really? What about your father? Had a healthy relationship with him, did you?"

Nick scowled at her, the color coming up in his face. "I hurt you and now you're trying to hurt me, but it won't make you feel any better."

"But I think I can fix you," Emmy said. "All I have to do is wave my magic wand and erase all the bad memories so you can be exactly what I want."

"I *wanted* your happiness."

Yeah, she'd hurt him, and he was right, it didn't make her feel any better. But it made her feel…solitary again. And that was her comfort zone. "The only thing that would make me happy is you walking out of my house."

"Fine," he said, "it's better than walking on eggshells with you." He turned when he got to the door, looked back at her. "I'm sorry for your past, Emmy. I'm sorry Roger was an ass, and I'm sorry you can't see what's right in front of you."

"I see what's in front of me, Nick," she said, "clearly, for the first time. That's what I'm sorry for."

Chapter Eighteen

Emmy drove to Porter and Son Tuesday morning, riding high on righteous anger and sheer determination. None of the employees came to the big bay door to stare out at her, even Stella's face was notably absent from the office window, and she greeted Emmy pleasantly when she walked in the front door. The rest of the week went downhill from there. By Friday she was on a first-name basis with Satan, her new landlord.

She'd gotten through the week because she refused not to. Burying herself in work helped, too. What time wasn't spent on the factory floor, she used to write her final report. It was lengthy, detailed and absolutely unnecessary, since there wasn't a chance in hell—her current residence—that Nick would put any of her suggestions into practice. Not that he'd told her as much, or that she'd given him the chance. Ignoring him worked pretty well, until Friday.

Friday she had to present her final recommendations and since there was no getting around the fact that it was going to make the last four days seem pleasant in comparison, she had no option but to put her head down and plow her way through this last meeting with Nick.

"I'm so glad you came in to talk," he said the minute Stella shut the door behind Emmy.

She dropped a copy of her report on his desk and took the seat in front of it, perching nervously on the edge. "Only about Porter and Son."

"Oh."

He sounded disappointed, but Emmy couldn't let her focus waver. Deliver the report and get out, that was her mantra. If she broke either of those rules, she'd be a mess, and there was no way she was going to burst into tears in front of Nick. It was chin up, spine stiff, all business. The way it always should have been.

"The new workflow is completed again," she said matter-of-factly, "thanks to Marty Henshaw." Marty had finally brought the rest of his compatriots into line, with Stella's help, Emmy assumed. Once everyone got with the program the rest of her job had been a piece of cake. "Your production schedule has been altered to allow for flexibility based on sales. I trained Stella on the new computer software so that when the orders come in she can purchase raw material more efficiently. That way you won't be sitting on inventory longer than necessary.

"Finished goods should be shipped immediately, with nothing going to the shelves so again—"

"We won't be sitting on inventory. I get it."

Emmy gave him a long, level look. She waited until he stopped smirking before she continued. "Inventory is one of your biggest expenses. Your products are fairly simple, so as long as you keep your lines adaptable, your costs should stay down." And if he chose to put everything back the way it was five minutes after she walked out the door, that was up to him.

"You did all this in four days?" Nick asked, paper rustling as he flipped through her report without waiting for her to guide him through it.

"It's amazing what can be accomplished when people cooperate."

More paper rustling, another moment of silence, then, "I can see how this will help," Nick said.

"Help," Emmy repeated so he'd get the nuance, "short-term. What's in this report will only delay the inevitable. There'll be a brief spike in profit, but if sales continue to decline, there won't be enough efficiency measures in the world to keep Porter and Son solvent.

"What you need is change, Nick, real, substantive modernization of your product line."

The silence drew out this time. Nick stared at her report, his jaw working. "We talked about this before, Emmy. I've tried to increase sales, but the market is pretty well tapped out."

"Fine."

That brought his eyes to hers. "Fine? All you have to say is fine? You've been dying to talk about this stuff since day one. I'm listening."

Emmy had promised herself she wouldn't try to sell Nick on ideas he'd already shot down, but he'd pushed one of her buttons. "You need to discontinue old products that aren't selling."

"If it's not selling we don't make it anymore."

"But it costs money to print in your catalog. If it's not selling stop advertising it."

"Fine," he said through clenched teeth.

Emmy resisted the urge to snap back at him the way he'd snapped at her. "You have finished product on the shelves that's been there since Elvis ate his first fried banana sandwich," she said, picking up with the next item on her list, and showing amazing—in her opinion—control. "Sell it."

"To?"

"Dollar stores, flea markets. You already patronize some charities, but you could do more of that as well. Every month you report that inventory as assets, and you pay taxes on it.

If you sell it, you take a loss, if you donate it you'll take a bigger loss, but at least you'll get the charity write-off. And you need to expand your product line."

"New products take new equipment."

"Then put in new equipment."

"We don't have the money for that."

"*You* have the money."

"My father set up my trust fund. Even if I could break the conditions of it, I wouldn't put my money into the business. Porter and Son needs to be self-sustaining."

"That's ridiculous." But Emmy let it go, partly because she didn't want to fight with Nick, mostly because she could give a rip about Porter and Son anymore. "Get an investor then."

Nick started to tell her why he couldn't do that. Emmy held up a hand. "Don't bother, I'm sure you have an argument against that, too. Why did you even hire me if you aren't interested in what I have to say?"

He didn't respond, unless looking miserable was a response, and strangely enough, she understood that better than any verbal reaction Nick might have had.

"Just tell me," she said.

If possible, he appeared even more miserable, but she had to give him credit, he didn't look away. And she had no trouble holding his gaze this time. Not when she was sure he was about to tell her something that would cut the professional legs right out from underneath her, just like he'd destroyed her personal foundations—what there were of them.

"I applied for a loan," he said as if he didn't realize how much it hurt her to hear him admit to yet another devastating secret. "The bank required a turnaround plan before they would approve it."

She got to her feet, wrapping her arms around herself as if she could keep out the pain, a futile attempt when the pain was already inside her. "At least it had nothing to do with me personally," she said, choosing to take him at his word and believe that he hadn't hired her because he was attracted to her. Maybe that was a foolish self-delusion, considering that he'd lied to her twice already, but it was also necessary if she was going to keep from falling apart until she was alone. Again. "It's your business Nick, do what you want."

"Change takes time."

"No it doesn't," Emmy countered, "it takes an open mind, the willingness to see that the market is different than it was thirty years ago, and the strength to make your people do what you tell them to. Because you're their boss."

"In other words, I'm a wimp who doesn't know how to run this company, and it's going to fail because of me. Where have I heard that before?" Nick stood, went to look out the window. "Oh, yeah, from my father."

Which made Emmy feel bad, for all of two seconds. He'd hired her to tell him what was wrong with his business. She wouldn't be doing her job if she wasn't honest with him, and she wouldn't handle him any differently because they'd slept together. Or because she'd fallen…

Nope, not going there.

She closed her heart, put her copy of the report back in her briefcase, and headed for the door. "I've done everything I can, Nick. The rest is up to you. If you insist on doing business the way your father did, if you won't change, you'll be closing your doors before the year is out."

Nick slapped her report down on his desk. "I can't. Don't you see? My father—"

"Your father was right," Emmy said, weary to the bottom of her heart and soul, so weary that all her good intentions flew out the window. "You can borrow enough money to fund a third-world nation, but it won't save Porter and Son. Not as long as you're so concerned about hurting feelings or laying people off that you won't force your employees to do what's right in order to save their jobs. You're still trying to change what you believe your father felt about you, and you can't because he's been gone for a long time. He's never going to take back what he said, he's never going to tell you he's proud of you, and you can't change the fact that you walked out that last time…"

Nick turned around slowly, and when his devastated eyes met hers, Emmy flinched.

"I'm sorry," she said, appalled when she realized what she'd said and how she'd said it. "I had no right." She moved toward the door, but she couldn't leave him like that. "You have to find a way to forgive yourself, or you'll always be living in your father's shadow, and you'll always feel like a failure."

"You didn't have parents, Emmy, you don't know what it's like. I can't just forget about my father."

She hadn't thought she could feel any more pain. She was wrong, so wrong that she had to let the hurt of Nick's words sink in for a second, until she could talk around it. About the tears in her eyes she could do nothing. "No, I didn't have parents, Nick, and it's something I never forget. Maybe when you think of your father you should try to remember the good moments, and not the way things ended between you. I doubt your father would have wanted you to torture yourself for the rest of your life."

He shoved a hand back through his hair. "Maybe you should keep your amateur psychoanalysis to yourself and do what I hired you to do, which is find a way to save this company."

"You didn't hire me to save the company," she shot back, "which is really too bad. I'd hate to see you lose this place. Porter and Son is the only thing I've ever seen you come close to taking seriously—"

"I took us seriously."

Emmy absorbed that like another blow, this one directly to the heart. "This is business, remember?"

Nick shrugged, but his jaw was still working, his eyes still stormy. "It's okay for you to cross the line, but not me?"

"Convincing my best friend to betray me wasn't crossing the line? Calling my foster families and having them ambush me wasn't crossing the line?" At some point during her tirade she must've stomped across the room, because she found herself standing in front of Nick, nearly toe to toe with him. The towering heat of her anger wouldn't let her back off. "If you think there's a line you haven't crossed, Nick, I don't know what the hell is stopping you now."

"You think I'm living in the past? You let your childhood turn you into a hermit. You think you're safe being alone, but you're not happy."

"And you are?"

"I was before…"

"Before I came along?" Emmy put some distance between them; she couldn't bear being near him anymore. The anger was gone, and without it to buffer her emotions there was only pain.

"I didn't mean it that way."

"Yes, you did. If you'd told me from the beginning all you wanted was a turnaround plan that you had no intention of actually implementing we could have avoided… everything else."

Nick came around the desk and put his hand on her arm. "I don't want it to end this way. I don't want it to end at all."

She shook her head, waited a moment until she was certain she could speak without giving in to her tears. "It's too late, Nick— No, let me finish before…" Before she threw up or cried or both. "When I took this job, I didn't realize

I'd be trespassing on the emotional issues you had with your father. You knew exactly what you were doing when you called my foster families, and you did it anyway. You can't just go around messing with someone's life that way."

"I just wanted to…to fix you."

"You did fix me," Emmy said, "for a little while at least. Just by being you and letting me be me."

Nick moved his hand away and stepped back to lean against his desk. Emmy didn't allow herself to recognize the emotion on his face as shock and devastation. If she let herself see that, let herself feel her own heart breaking, she wouldn't be able to say what needed to be said so she could put Nick Porter in her past, where he belonged.

"You were all I needed, Nick. I fell in love with you. That's not easy for me to admit, but you were the first person—" She swallowed to ease the tightness in her throat. "I thought you were first person, the first man, who ever loved me for who I am."

"I do," Nick insisted. "I fell in love with you the minute I saw you."

Emmy picked up her briefcase again, the weight of it comforting, steadying. "There's no such thing as love at first sight."

"Don't tell me how I feel."

"What you felt when you met me, that was only chemistry."

"We definitely have that," Nick muttered.

"It's not enough. This," Emmy indicated her hair, her face, "isn't me. I'm inside here, the heart, the brain, the flaws."

"I know that."

"Then why did you try to change me? Why didn't you just let our relationship grow, let me take this slowly until I trusted myself, because I trusted you not to hurt me."

"God, Emmy, I could see how unhappy you were, how—"

"Wounded? Nobody has a perfect childhood, Nick. We're all shaped by our circumstances, and you're right that I was letting mine have way too much influence over my life. I'll try my best not to judge everyone I meet by the past anymore, and for that I'm grateful to you."

"That's all, just grateful?"

"Goodbye." She turned her back and walked to the door, kept going even after Nick called her back. Their business, personal and professional, was done.

There was nothing left to talk about. But she didn't think she'd be putting this one in her job-well-done column.

Chapter Nineteen

"You don't look surprised to see me," Lindy said when Emmy swung her front door open.

"I could tell it was you from the way you rang the doorbell. There's an attitude."

"The doorbell has an attitude when I ring it? That's BS."

"Then how did I know it was you?"

Lindy scowled at her. "There are any number of responses to that, but calling you names won't help my case."

Emmy leaned against the edge of the door. "Your case?"

Lindy brushed by her. "My plea to get you to forgive me."

"Forgive you for what?"

That brought Lindy to a halt. Halfway to the living room, she swung around. "You don't know about what Nick and I did?"

Emmy sent her a long, steady look. "I didn't think you knew that I knew."

"I, uh…well, you see…"

She almost laughed. Lindy Masterson, cool, calm litigator was actually stammering and embarrassed. At a loss, is how Emmy would have described her. "Your face is a pretty interesting shade of red," she observed mildly.

"Dammit, Emmy! Nick called me, all right?"

"Don't they call that fraternizing with the enemy in your profession?"

"Only if my profession involved artillery and saluting. The army," Lindy explained when Emmy only frowned at her. "The point is, I'm sorry." She stuffed the gift bag she was holding into Emmy's hands. "I brought you coffee and chocolate. Really expensive coffee and chocolate," she said. "And they're not mixed together because I remembered how you got sick on the chocolate-covered coffee beans, and whenever I eat something and then throw up I can never eat it again, or in my case drink it. Take tequila for instance, I got sick as a dog on tequila in law school and I haven't touched it since. And then there's—"

"Lindy," Emmy said, loud enough to cut through, "you're rambling."

"I know, but I can't help myself because I'm afraid if I stop talking you'll tell me to get lost and I really don't want you to tell me to get lost. You have to forgive me, Emmy. Nick called and told me you knew what I did, and I waited for you to call me, but you didn't so here I am."

Emmy thought about that a minute. "I just have one question. How in the world did he talk you into it?"

Lindy huffed out a breath that blew her bangs off her forehead. "Have you ever gone head to head with him? Never mind, obviously you have. The man should be a lawyer, that's all I'm saying. I tried to talk him out of it, but he shot down all my arguments and before I knew it I was agreeing to help him. I know what I did was wrong, but I did it for you."

"I forgive you *because* you did it for me."

"Really?" Lindy seemed to slump, all the tension draining out of her. "Really?"

"Really." Emmy felt her lips curving upward. It was a small smile, and it contained a good amount of sarcasm, but it was the first time she'd smiled and really felt it in over a week. Since she'd walked out on Nick, the lying, manipulating scumbag she was in love with.

Lindy threw her arms around Emmy, the gift bag crushed between them. "Nick wanted what was best for you, too, Emmy."

"No, he did it for himself." Emmy stepped back and led the way into the living room. "I'm not good enough for Nick the way I am, Lindy. If I was he wouldn't have wanted to change me."

"He didn't want to change you. He just didn't have the patience to wait for you to get there on your own. That's what happens when you love someone. You want that person to love you back immediately."

Emmy had lost her appetite a week ago, the same time she'd lost her smile. But she needed something to take her mind off Nick. Since she wasn't depressed enough to drink on an empty stomach, chocolate was the only mood-altering substance left, and it was conveniently handy.

"I was wrong, Emmy," Lindy said into the silence. "I never should have let Nick talk me into helping him, but I understand why he did it."

"Water under the bridge."

Lindy flopped onto the sofa, shaking her head when Emmy held out the box of chocolates. "You need to be sure," she said.

Emmy didn't need to ask what she was supposed to be sure of. "I've thought about nothing else for most of the week." She'd examined what had happened between her and Nick, the right and the wrong, and while she knew it was too soon to be completely objective, she thought she'd done a pretty good job of holding on to the former and beginning to let go of the latter. No way was she going to forget the things she'd learned about herself, or turn her back on what she'd realized she wanted. That meant she couldn't allow the heartbreak to get in her way. But she needed some time to get over it before she could risk again. "I'm sure."

"You know, Nick called me the day after your fight—"

"Lindy…"

"Just let me have my say, and then I promise I'll never bring him up again."

"Fine, Nick called you because he wanted your help. That's what he does, Lindy. Whenever there's something unpleasant, he lets someone else handle it for him."

"It's not like that. He wanted to make sure your foster records were resealed."

"It's the least he could do, considering it's his fault they were opened in the first place. And it wasn't opening the records that caused the problem anyway. It was being ambushed by my past every time I turned around. Can he fix that? Can you?"

"Nick is really torn up," Lindy said, looking pretty miserable herself, but sticking to her guns—or contracts since she didn't appreciate military references. "Why don't you go talk to him, Emmy? Let him apologize, if nothing else."

"An apology isn't going to change anything." Which was why she hadn't taken any of his phone calls, returned any of his messages, and had refused delivery of the flowers he'd sent her. She didn't want any more contact with Nick, and that included hearing his name.

"Nick—"

"Stop. Please, just stop."

Lindy swallowed her words back and stared, eyes wide, hands clenched tightly together in her lap.

Emmy spun around and stomped into the kitchen, snapping at her best friend was the last straw. Lindy followed her, and Emmy knew she saw her wiping her eyes, but like the true friend she was, Lindy didn't comment on it. "I'm sorry," Emma said.

"Me, too." Lindy took a stool at the counter. "I never know when to butt out. I won't talk about Nick anymore, but I'm going to talk about you, Emmy, and I'm not letting you kick me out until I'm done."

Emmy opened the refrigerator, and although it was always ruthlessly organized she made a show of rooting around inside. Her nerves were pretty raw, her emotions right on the surface, but she knew that tone of voice. Lindy wasn't going anywhere until she'd had her say. When Emmy felt steady enough, she retrieved a couple of bottled waters and handed one to her best friend.

"Thanks but no thanks," Lindy said, "unless you've got some whiskey to go along with this."

"The last thing I need right now is to get drunk and sloppy."

"It might do you good," Lindy observed, then let the subject go. It seemed like the right time for out-of-character actions, so she took a fortifying swig of water and jumped in with both feet. "Hold on to yourself, because this is the touchy-feely part of the program."

Emmy took a long drink herself. "Shoot."

"Still stuck on those military references." Lindy rolled her eyes, and Emmy smiled a little, both of them relaxing. For a second or two.

"I've known you since we were roommates in college," Lindy began. "That's a long time for two people who aren't what you'd call relationship-ready to be friends.

"You've changed, though. Maybe it wasn't Nick, but you've, I don't know, let go. You took a risk, Emmy."

"Yeah, that was a real success."

"Look, maybe it didn't work out, but don't let it send you…"

"Running?" Emmy came around the counter and took a stool. "I'm not running away, Lindy. I'm just…" Wounded, hurting. Devastated. "It's only been a week. I can't get involved with anyone right now, but it won't always be that way."

Lindy didn't appear to be convinced. Emmy wasn't all that sure herself. It was easy to say it; *give the pain time to fade and then take a chance with someone new.* It wouldn't be so easy to do, but with a little effort she could make herself believe there would be a time when she could open up again, find someone else and have a home and family of her own. At the moment it was the only fairy tale she was interested in.

"Emmy, what if Nick walked through your front door and said all the right things?"

"He did say all the right things. But it wasn't the words, Lindy. Anyone can say the words, but not everyone can back them up, and it's the actions that really matter."

Lindy considered that for a moment, then smiled slightly. "I guess you really did learn something. Maybe Nick did, too."

"Not likely," Emmy said with a soft, derisive laugh. "He's just as locked in the past as I used to be, and he doesn't seem the least bit inclined to change that."

"And if he did? If he found a way to prove it to you?"

Emmy shrugged. "I'm hardly hiding from him. I've been right here all week, but he's chosen phone calls and deliverymen over face-to-face. I'm not expecting him to make a reappearance in my life, but if he did I wouldn't avoid him, either. And get that look off your face," she added. "I'm not holding the foster thing against you, but if you call Nick, we're through."

"Yeah, I figured that out for myself. And anyway you can't send me packing. You wouldn't have any friends left."

"I'll get new friends," Emmy said, not completely joking. "I've made all this progress, remember?"

NICK HAD CALLED Emmy and left messages. She hadn't called him back. He'd sent flowers; she'd refused delivery. That only made him angrier, even when he admitted she'd been right about the company, and about his father, he was still too angry to do anything about it.

A week later he was too exhausted to be angry anymore. He wasn't sleeping, he wasn't eating, and Porter and Son could have fallen off the face of the earth for all he cared. All he had left was heartache, which he didn't think would ever go away since the depth of his pain was directly proportional to the depth of his love for Emmy.

There was only one solution; he had to get her back. The question was, how? He'd replayed their argument a hundred times, looked at it from every possible angle, and the part that stood out was the sheer determination on Emmy's face when she'd walked out his door. And out of his life.

She'd meant every word she'd said. She was through with him. And still he was holding out hope because the minute Stella walked in and told him he had a visitor Nick was out of his chair like a shot. He stopped short in his office doorway, frowning at the man who stepped over and held out his hand.

Nick took it, zoning out for a second when the guy introduced himself. "Did you say Joe Esterhaus?"

"He wouldn't tell me his name or what he wanted," Stella whispered, sending Joe a look of patent displeasure.

"It's all right." Nick stepped back and gestured Joe Esterhaus into his office. "Emmy's not here," he said, waiting until Stella took a seat at her desk before he closed the door. He didn't want to hold this conversation with the possibility she'd have her ear pressed to the door.

"I didn't come to see Emmy," Joe said, ignoring the chair

Nick indicated, walking to the window instead. "And anyway, I got your message. You don't want me to see her."

"So you came to see me instead? Why?"

Joe turned around, studied Nick long enough to make him uncomfortable. "You're in love with her, aren't you?"

"That's none—"

"Sure, none of my business. I know that. I also know you wouldn't go to all this trouble to get through to her if you didn't love her."

"Fat lot of good it did me," Nick muttered, collapsing into his chair.

"I had a crush…" Joe came over and took the seat opposite Nick's desk. "No, *crush* is too mild a word to describe how I felt about Emmy, and I need to go back further.

"I was an only child, and my mother always wanted more kids," he began again, "a daughter to be exact, but by the time my parents stopped trying to have one of their own I was heading into my teenage years, and Mom didn't think it would be fair to me to adopt or bring a foster child into the house. So, she waited until I was eighteen and headed off to college.

"Emmy was sixteen when she came to live with us. I was home an occasional weekend and holidays, like every other college kid. She was nothing to me but a visitor in the beginning. But that first summer when I came home, well, there's something about her. I can't put it into words."

"You don't have to."

"No, for you I guess I don't. In any case, to make a long story short, I fell hard for her, but by the second summer she was eighteen and headed off to college herself. She'd never given me a second look, and I didn't really know what to do or what to say."

Joe looked toward the window again. "Once Emmy left she never came back. It made my mother sad, but she took in other kids after that, and I went back to college and got on with my life. Looking back now, if I had been older, or more mature, I would have realized how hard it must have been for Emmy to be shuttled from one home to another her whole life." He shifted his gaze to Nick again. "I would have tried harder to get through to her."

Nick felt his jaw working, but he held the other man's gaze. "You have a point?"

"I have regrets," Joe said, "that's my point."

"You're married."

Joe stared down at the gold band on his left ring finger. "Probably not for long. That's going to be another regret. But I'll tell you this. Some day I'm going to look up Emmy Jones again."

Nick didn't ask him if that was a warning. It felt more like a threat. One look at the guy, tall and blond and built as though he spent a third of every day at the gym, and Nick knew he was trouble. He hadn't done all that work and all that suffering to help Emmy come to terms with her past in order for Joe Esterhaus, or any other man, to step in and reap all the rewards.

But Emmy wasn't going to forget everything, just because Nick asked her to. He had to convince her he'd changed. The trouble was, he didn't know how to do that.

By the time he remembered he wasn't alone, he was. Joe Esterhaus had taken his leave sometime during Nick's private recap of the impossible situation he'd gotten himself into. Unfortunately Stella and Marty Henshaw decided to take Joe's place. "There's no chance we could do...whatever this is later?" he asked them.

"It's too late already," Stella announced, dropping into one of the chairs in front of Nick's desk and motioning Marty, sharply, to take the other. "Your efficiency expert was right," she said when everyone was arranged to her satisfaction and appropriately attentive. "If you don't make changes Porter and Son will go bankrupt."

Stella waited for one of the two men to have some input—approximately the same amount of time it took her to draw breath—and then she continued. "If you don't set this place to rights and get it headed for success, we're all quitting."

Marty's contribution was to nod vigorously.

"You're threatening me?" Nick asked.

"If we must," Stella said. "Emmy Jones is right. It's time to let the past go. Your father was a hard man. He wasn't always like that, but he missed your mother so desperately…I don't think he really knew how to go on without her."

For the first time Nick could see things from his father's side. Because of Emmy. He could understand all too well how it must have felt to lose the woman you loved. He'd been without Emmy for a week, and he was already going crazy. His father had lost his mother forever.

"He didn't mean those things he said to you, or to treat you so badly," Stella was saying. "He was hurting and angry, and he took it out on you more than anyone else. Don't let it dictate how you live your life. This company isn't more important than your happiness."

Marty had disappeared into the reception area when the conversation strayed into the personal. When he came back he was carrying the suggestion box, which he dropped on Nick's desk.

"Um…why don't you start without me," Nick suggested. "I have an errand to run."

He knew what he had to do now. Not because of Joe Esterhaus or his employees' demands—okay, maybe Joe had helped him come to the conclusion that some sort of grand gesture was going to be required to get Emmy back. And maybe Stella had pushed him that last inch into absolute clarity of mind. Whatever the catalyst, suddenly his course of action was crystal clear. It felt good, it felt right, and it was the scariest thing he'd ever faced in his life.

But it wasn't scarier than living without Emmy.

Chapter Twenty

The second week A.N. (after Nick) was a tiny bit easier than the first, mainly because Emmy kept busy. She'd started working for the client she'd had lunch with right before she and Nick had spent those amazing five days together... And if she didn't stop measuring her life in terms of Nick she'd drive herself absolutely crazy.

Marcus Higgins, her new client, always dressed appropriately, always kept his demeanor businesslike, and still managed to make it clear that he wouldn't be averse to a relationship outside of the office. Emmy didn't have any trouble staying on the correct side of the business/personal line—or keeping him from crossing it.

Marcus owned a small business, just like Nick. Otherwise they couldn't have been more different than fish and birds. Marcus listened to all her ideas, and not just because he had ulterior motives. He really wanted to improve his company's bottom line. He knew how to motivate his employees, so they were all behind her one hundred percent. And he had no personal issues that presented impediments to her performing the duties for which she'd been contracted. In short, Marcus Higgins was a dream client.

Emmy hated him.

No, *hate* was too strong. More like she couldn't wait to finish the job and put Marcus in her past.

His smile didn't make her all warm and fluttery inside, for one thing. He didn't have an irreverent sense of humor, or a way of looking at her that made her feel like the center of the universe. And she suspected kissing Marcus would feel like the time she'd practiced on her mirror in junior high school, cold and passionless and unsatisfying—at least on her side. In fact, she couldn't imagine ever kissing anyone but Nick again.

And she imagined she'd get over it. In time. Lots and lots of time. What else did she have but time?

She picked up her coffee cup and sipped, looking out over the open square her favorite coffee shop faced. The square was surrounded by shops and small restaurants, many of them still closed. Tables and chairs studded the open space, which was practically empty. Just the way Emmy liked it. It was early yet, the sun still shining through the branches of the trees planted in little cut-out holes in the concrete. A few work-bound pedestrians were buying coffee, juggling the hot cups with their briefcases and newspapers.

Emmy sat at her favorite table and watched the world go by. She'd avoided it since she'd run into Jerry there, but she wasn't letting anyone chase her away from anything ever again. Running, unless it was for exercise, was something she intended to give up completely.

She was taking things at a slower pace from now on, too. Relaxation, it was called, living life to the fullest, taking time to smell the roses. Work might be all she had in her life right now, but she wasn't filling her life up with work to the exclusion of all else. She was going to take time off, and work normal hours, and find a hobby. Maybe.

Mostly she was determined to get comfortable with herself. She'd always believed she spent so much time alone because she liked her own company. Big, fat lie. The reality was, she spent hardly any time with herself. She didn't even like her own thoughts, particularly, not when they concerned her personal life—or threatened to take her on a trip down memory lane. She'd buried herself in work so she didn't have time to think, or notice how lonely she was, or how much it hurt to see a happy family, or a couple holding hands. Or anyone with love in their life.

Building walls, she admitted to herself, was her special talent. Building walls was the driving force behind every decision she'd made since she'd been old enough to make them. The sterile neighborhood she lived in, the lines she drew in her personal life, starting her own business. Especially starting her own business. Not only did she get to work herself to exhaustion, but self-employment meant no bosses or co-workers or mail-room clerks. She didn't have to get tangled up in anyone's life, because you couldn't work with someone on a regular basis and not get tangled up. And once she was tangled up, once there were weekend barbecues and family photos on desks, she'd be faced every day with what was missing from her life.

Well, she was alone, exactly the way she'd wanted it, but she'd discovered what was missing from her life anyway. Herself. And she intended to reestablish contact, even if it meant getting in touch with some less-than-attractive parts of her own personality.

She drank some coffee, smiling a little. It sounded brave, proactive. It was more a matter of degrees. After what she'd been through in Nick's office that last time, she could survive anything.

Except maybe Nick. Striding across the square. Headed for her.

Emmy had two choices, run or stay put, and since she was

frozen in place, and running wasn't really an option, she decided to stay where she was.

Nick decided to sit down across from her, and stare hungrily at her face. Thank God he wasn't smiling, was all she could think, because if he smiled she'd throw herself across the table and right into his arms, and to hell with pride, or her broken heart, or making sure he understood that if they were going to have any kind of relationship he needed to understand what had gone wrong the first time. So they could keep it from happening again.

"Are you going to talk to me?"

She took a few more seconds—a pitifully short time—to get herself under control, but she wasn't about to let Nick know how hard her heart was beating, and how much she hoped…Even she couldn't bear to know the extent of it.

"However did you know I'd be here?" she finally said, and despite the fact that her attempt at humor fell flat, some of her confidence returned when her voice sounded almost normal.

He didn't say anything, just placed an envelope on the table in front of her. Through the little window on the front of it, Emmy could tell it was a check.

The hope she'd been unable to guard against died.

"I know I said I only hired you to satisfy my bankers," he continued when she didn't pick up the check, "but after you left my employees had a change of heart. They told me if I didn't make changes, they were quitting."

"Good for them," she said, her heart like a stone in her chest, a cold dead stone that made the flesh around it ache.

"So you really earned this." Nick nudged the envelope closer to her side of the table.

She didn't so much as glance at it. "It sounds to me like your employees earned it."

"Because of you. It took a while, but you finally convinced them you were right."

Emmy smiled faintly. "They weren't the ones who needed convincing."

"You convinced me, too," Nick said, as if that went without saying.

Emmy could have told him that was half the reason they were in their current predicament, and if he'd figured it out, oh, about two weeks ago they might not have broken up. But it wouldn't mean anything if she had to tell him what he'd done wrong. And anyway, she thought as she tuned back into the conversation, it didn't really matter anymore. That check was the last straw.

Once she'd discovered why Nick had really hired her, she'd never felt that she'd earned her fee. His using it as an excuse to see her—

"I know what you're thinking," he said.

She smiled slightly. "I was thinking you could have mailed it."

"But then I wouldn't have had a chance to apologize." Nick leaned forward, the hand that reached across the table stopped just short of taking hers. "I didn't tell you about the bank loan, Emmy, and I'm sorry, but the truth is, if I'd hired another consultant, I still would have kept it to myself."

"Why?" she asked, truly puzzled, and still just a little hopeful.

Nick shrugged. "I didn't want you to feel like all your hard work was useless."

"But it was," Emmy said, although she took care to make sure there was no sting of resentment in her voice. Nick was considerate to a fault, and whether it was because he didn't want to hurt anyone's feelings or to save himself any upheaval didn't matter. The important point was that she believed his reason for hiding the truth about his intentions. "If you'd told me you only wanted some recommendations, that's all I would have provided. I wouldn't have pushed so hard for you to make changes."

"If you hadn't I never would have figured out where I was going wrong, and neither would my employees," Nick said. "I was so tied up in proving my father wrong I was willing to let things continue the way they were going until the company failed."

"I'm glad you changed your mind."

"That's not all," he said, sitting forward, all proud of himself and smiling. Totally clueless.

"Once I get the company back on its feet, thanks to your turnaround plan, I'll arrange for my employees to buy me out for a reasonable price. It's always been their place more than mine anyway."

Emmy stared at him a minute while she let the meaning of his announcement sink in. She'd been trying to get him to face the truth for almost a month, and he'd fought her every step of the way. And sure, she understood it was because he'd been hurting over his father, but why did he have to cause himself—and her—so much pain before he got it? And why did he think that making decisions, even long-overdue ones, about Porter and Son would make a difference now?

But those were questions she couldn't bring herself to ask. Or maybe she wasn't ready for the answers. "You're walking away?" she asked instead. "Just like that?"

"It won't be just like that. The transition will take a while, and I promised to stay on until they can pick up the front-office stuff. But then I'm free."

"To do what?"

Nick did a hands-up. "I don't know."

Now there, she thought, was the Nick she knew and—

"I'm not sure what I want to do for the rest of my life,"

Nick said, saving Emmy from the dangerous and painful path of her own thoughts, "but it finally occurred to me that the reason I'm not motivated is because Porter and Son isn't what I want. It never has been. After my father died I took over because…" he spread his hands. "You know the reasons as well as I do.

"When I find the right career, Emmy, something that *I* want, you won't recognize me." He reached for her hand, curling his fingers into a fist when she pulled back before he could make contact. "And if you're not there, it won't matter what I do. Nothing will matter."

"Nick—"

"No, let me finish. I made a pretty good start at figuring things out after our argument, but it still took Stella to fill in the rest of the blanks. She told me how devastated my father was when my mother died, and after our argument, the thought of never seeing you again… I could understand how he felt, how much he must have missed my mother. When I realized he had to live with that the rest of his life, it wasn't hard to see why he changed so drastically, why he became so hard.

"You were right that I was waiting for my dad to forgive me, but I had to forgive him, too. I won't say I'm a hundred percent there yet, but I think I'm on my way."

Nick sat there, looking so hopeful that Emmy wished she could say what he wanted to hear. She couldn't because he hadn't said what *she* needed to hear. "I'm glad you've made peace with your memories, Nick."

He kept his eyes on her another minute, then looked away. "This isn't going the way I expected."

"What did you expect?" she shot back, still hurt and angry with it. "Did you think you could just show up out of the blue, give me a progress report, and I'd throw myself into your arms?"

"Did I tell you how sorry I was?" But his smile faded when she failed to be amused. "I'm sorry, Emmy, for everything."

"So am I."

Nick watched her look out over the square. It was still as empty as it had been ten minutes before, but the peace that had been on her face when he'd first spotted her sitting alone was gone. And it was his fault.

He wracked his brain, but he couldn't for the life of him figure out where he'd gone wrong. He'd apologized, more than once. He'd explained about his father, and the company, and the decisions he'd made after what he'd learned about both. And he'd told her— Damn, how could he forget that?

"I love you," he said.

Her gaze swiveled back to his, held for a few seconds while the silence grew heavier. "I'm happy that you're moving on," she finally said, "and I hope it works out, Nick, really I do—"

"But you aren't waiting around to find out." He crossed his arms and sat back in his chair. It was the hardest thing he'd ever done when what he really wanted was to knock the table out of his way, take her in his arms and force her to give him the words he wanted to hear. "That's not acceptable."

Emmy huffed out a little breath. "What?"

"When you took this job you promised to fix my company."

"Well, it sounds like it's all fixed," Emmy pointed out. "You said so yourself. And you paid me." She picked up the check and stuffed it carelessly into her purse.

Nick thought he saw her hands shaking, and his heart slammed against the inside of his ribcage, racing with the knowledge that he might be able to reach her, after everything he'd done, she might still love him. "I need help to make Porter and Son stable again," he said. "I need you."

Emmy shook her head. "You've discovered your problem, Nick, and you're well on the way to fixing yourself."

"But I might backslide. How will you know if you don't stick around?"

"This isn't about business."

"No. It's about you and me. It's about the fact that we love each other but you're trying to walk away. Well, I'm not taking no for an answer, and I'll do whatever it takes to make you admit that we belong together."

"That's what got you in trouble the first time," Emmy reminded him.

Nick took a deep breath and let it out, not because patience was getting thin. Because hope was. He couldn't remember Emmy ever being so reserved. Sure, she'd made a big deal out of being professional, but there'd always been a spark, a kind of light that shone from her, even when she was trying to be severe with him.

Now that light was…not extinguished, but definitely dimmed. Nick had to shoulder the blame for that, and it was up to him to make it right again. "I'll wait, no matter how long it takes."

"Hanging around where you're not wanted sort of makes you a stalker," Emmy said.

Not wanted. That would have hurt if he hadn't written her bluntness off to the hurt and frustration he heard in her voice. "So there's no hope?"

"No." But she wouldn't look at him, and when he reached over and curled his hand around her wrist, he felt her pulse spike. "I'm not the reason your heart is beating double-time?"

She moved her hand away.

"I didn't realize I'd hurt you that much," Nick said.

Emmy looked as though she might deny that, then bumped one shoulder up. "You did," she said. "It was bad enough tha

I didn't trust myself, but, it was worse to find out that you didn't trust me, either."

"I know. I get it. I should have let our relationship progress the way it was supposed to, in its own way. It's just that I fell in love with you the moment I saw you. For the first time in my life I was in a hurry."

"So you decided to force me to catch up by bringing those…people back into my life?"

"I wanted to help you."

"You wanted to change me." She looked away, but not before Nick saw the tears in her eyes.

That got to him most of all, her tears, the more so because she tried to hide them. It would have taken a blind man not to see the depth of her pain, but he had been blind, Nick realized. He'd wanted words when any fool could see she'd already shown him by her actions how deeply her feelings ran. She'd let him drag her out of her self-imposed isolation, despite the fact that he knew how hard it was for her to open up to anyone. Then, when he needed help, she'd tried to make him see that she wasn't the only one being kept a prisoner by her past. And he'd savaged her for it.

"God, Emmy," Nick said, rubbing at the ache in his chest, "I'm sorry I didn't understand. You were trying to help me—"

Emmy took to her feet and strode off across the square. Nick kept pace with her, but he stuffed his hands in his pockets before the urge to touch her, to drag her into his arms, became too much to resist. She wasn't ready for that yet. And he'd learned that her pace mattered as much as his.

"I only wanted you to be happy," he said. "With me, sure, but that wasn't the bottom line. I contacted your foster families for your sake. You don't have to believe me, but I was prepared to stay away from you, at least until you'd had time to understand what your childhood had done to you. But then we…I knew I was in love with you and I couldn't keep my distance.

"And you're wrong that I didn't trust you."

She glanced over at him, but she kept walking.

"If I hadn't trusted you, do you think I'd have risked helping you heal only to lose you? If I didn't really love you, Emmy, I wouldn't want you to grow. It would be better for me if you didn't, because that way you'd never leave."

She halted in mid stride, but she didn't look at him. "Like Roger."

Nick hadn't said that, but he'd hoped she'd make the comparison. "I want what's best for you. Even if it's not best for me. If that means you have to walk away—"

She spun around and punched him in the arm. "Dammit, Nick." She punched him again. But there were tears in her eyes.

He took it slowly, wrapping his arms around her, half afraid she'd try to push him away. Instead she sighed and rested her forehead against his shoulder. "Lindy was right," she said, "you should be a lawyer."

"But?"

"I don't know, Nick."

"That's because you're still afraid."

She leaned back and looked up at him.

"It's why you left in the first place," he explained. "Yes, I did some things wrong, and I hurt you, and I'm sorry for that. But if you'll just take one more chance, Emmy, I'll never hurt you again— Okay, I'll probably hurt you again, but I'll never lie to you. And I'll wait, no matter how long it takes…"

"Is it my turn to talk now?"

Nick nodded, looking pretty miserable.

"You're right, I am afraid. I figured that out weeks ago, right after the charity fair."

"And then I gave you even more reason to be afraid."

Emmy put her fingers over his lips, ignoring the tingle. "I'm willing to try again," she said, "I have to."

"Because?"

The feel of his lips moving against her skin was enough to make her forget how much was at stake. She held on to her wits, if not her breath. It was an important moment. Life-altering. "I love you," she said.

It took a minute for her words to sink in, then Nick smiled and warmth spilled through her. It was just like the first time he'd smiled at her, only this time there was a lightness, a boundless joy that was the weight of her past lifting, at last, off her heart and soul. Love welled up in her, with a depth that couldn't be measured.

"Will you marry me?" Nick asked.

She threw her arms around his neck, laughing as he whirled her off her feet. When he set her back down and his mouth met hers, it felt as if she was still spinning. She put her hands on his shoulders and opened her eyes, looking deeply into his.

"Well?"

"Maybe," she said laughing. "Not today—or tomorrow," she added when he looked like he might suggest just that, "but some day."

Nick spun her again and set her down, framing her face in his hands and kissing her with such softness and respect that she knew it wouldn't be long before she gave in and married him. And as scary as that was, she couldn't wait.

Silhouette® Desire

NEW YORK TIMES BESTSELLING AUTHOR

DIANA PALMER

A brand-new Long, Tall Texans novel

IRON COWBOY

*Available March 2008
wherever you buy books.*

Texas Hold 'Em

When it comes to love, the stakes are high

Sixteen years ago, Luke Chisum dated
Becky Parker on a dare…before going
on to break her heart. Now the former
River Bluff daredevil is back, rekindling
desire and tempting Becky to pick up
where they left off. But this time she has
to resist or Luke could discover the secret
she's kept locked away all these years.…

Look for

TEXAS BLUFF

by Linda Warren

#1470

*Available February 2008
wherever you buy books.*

HSR71470

$1.00 OFF

The bestselling Lakeshore Chronicles continue with *Snowfall at Willow Lake*, a story of what comes after a woman survives an unspeakable horror and finds her way home, to healing and redemption and a new chance at happiness.

SUSAN WIGGS

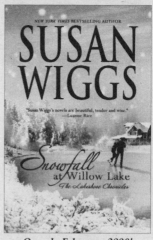

On sale February 2008!

SAVE $1.00

off the purchase price of **SNOWFALL AT WILLOW LAKE** by **Susan Wiggs.**

Offer valid from February 1, 2008, to April 30, 2008.
Redeemable at participating retail outlets. Limit one coupon per purchase.

52608168

5 65373 00076 2   (8100) 0 11463

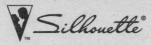

Romantic
SUSPENSE

**Sparked by Danger,
Fueled by Passion.**

When Tech Sergeant Jacob "Mako" Stone opens
his door to a mysterious woman without a past,
he knows his time off is over. As threats to Dee's
life bring her and Jacob together, she must set
aside her pride and accept the help of the military
hero with too many secrets of his own.

Out of Uniform
by Catherine Mann

Available February wherever you buy books.

SRS27571

You can lead a horse to water…

When Alyssa Barkley and Clint Westmoreland
found out that their "fake" marriage was never
rendered void, they are forced to live together
for thirty days. However, Clint loves the single
life and has no intention of being tamed, but
when Alyssa moves in, the sizzling attraction
between them is ignited and neither wants the
thirty days to end.

Look for

TAMING CLINT WESTMORELAND

by

BRENDA JACKSON

Available February wherever you buy books

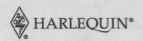

HARLEQUIN®

American ★ Romance®

COMING NEXT MONTH

#1197 THE FAMILY PLAN by Cathy McDavid
Fatherhood

It's an emotional homecoming for injured show rider Jolyn Sutherland...
especially when she runs into veterinarian Chase Raintree, her secret
girlhood crush. This time around, he seems to return the feeling. But a crisis
involving Jolyn's family and Chase's eight-year-old daughter could derail their
relationship before it gets off the ground....

#1198 UNEXPECTED BRIDE by Lisa Childs
The Wedding Party

Only her best friend's wedding could bring Abby Hamilton back to her Michigan
hometown. But when the bride runs away, sparks fly between Abby and Clayton
McClintock, a man she always admired...even when he thought she was nothing
but trouble. Could it be that the people of Cloverdale will get to see a wedding
after all?

#1199 THE RIGHT MR. WRONG by Cindi Myers

Everyone in Crested Butte, Colorado, has warned Maddie Alexander about the
good-looking Hagan Ansdar. His no-commitment views make him an *in*eligible
bachelor. Good thing she's immune to Mr. Wrong...or is she? Because when
Hagan pursues her, she finds it hard to resist!

#1200 IN A SOLDIER'S ARMS by Marin Thomas
Hearts of Appalachia

When Maggie O'Neil goes home to the family birthplace, Heather's Hollow,
she's expecting to find out all the clan's secrets from a grandmother who claims
every O'Neil woman has "second sight." Maggie doesn't believe a word of
it—until she meets ex-soldier Abram Devane and "sees" her future—with him!

www.eHarlequin.com

HARCNM0108